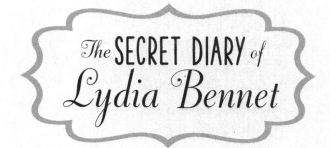

The SECRET DIARY of
Lydia Bennet

ALSO BY NATASHA FARRANT

After Iris

Following Flora

What We Did for Love

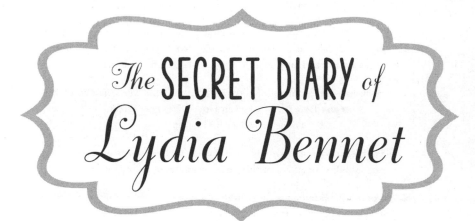

The SECRET DIARY of Lydia Bennet

NATASHA FARRANT

Chicken House

SCHOLASTIC INC. | NEW YORK

Library of Congress Cataloging-in-Publication Number : 2016012705

ISBN 978-0-545-94031-3

10 9 8 7 6 5 4 3 2 1   16 17 18 19 20

Printed in the U.S.A. 23

First edition, November 2016

Book design by Abby Dening

For Elinor

Hertfordshire, 1811

BUT REALLY DECADES BEHIND THE MODERN WORLD
BECAUSE WE ARE IN
THE DEPTHS OF THE ENGLISH COUNTRYSIDE
WHERE
NOTHING
<u>EVER</u>
HAPPENS

THURSDAY, 13TH JUNE

I am fifteen years old today, and this journal was a present from Mary. She says I must write in it every day to improve my mind.

"Whatever for," Mamma cried, "when she is so pretty?"

Father asked, "Are we even certain Lydia *has* a mind?"

"Of course she does!" Mary said. "It's just not very developed."

"Excuse me!" I tried to look down my nose at her, which was not easy because I was sitting and she was standing. "Right now, my undeveloped mind thinks you are extremely rude."

Mamma snatched the diary out of my hand and waved it

about like a murder weapon. "You had much better have given her some ribbon! She is so clever at making things."

"What should I write about?" I asked, retrieving the diary.

"Reflections and meditations," Mary murmured. "Prayers. Observations. The opposite of your usual frivolities."

"I am not frivolous," I snarled.

Father cried, "Ha!" and left the room.

"You are a *bit*," Kitty said.

"Just write down what you do each day, dear." Jane frowned at Kitty and Mary, urging them to be nice.

"And how it makes you feel," Lizzy added.

∽≥◌

So, to begin!

For breakfast, Hill made my favorite sweet rolls, with fresh cream and raspberry jam, which made me happy. Then my sisters gave me my presents in order of age, as always, from the oldest to the youngest.

Jane gave me some lace to trim my new sprigged muslin. This also made me happy. Jane always gives the prettiest things.

Lizzy gave me a yellow ribbon for my bonnet, which made me cross because she knows I wanted the lilac.

Mary gave me this journal (and I have already said quite enough about *that*).

Kitty gave me a needlepoint cushion. "Lord knows what you will do with it," she said, "but cushions are the only thing I

4

know how to make. You needn't pretend to like it." So I didn't, but then one of the new tabby kittens kneaded it with his tiny claws, clambered onto it with his tiny legs, and fell asleep with tiny snores. It is a perfect kitten bed. Kitty and I carried him up to our room. We have called him Napoleon, because he is small but already tyrannical. And so the cushion was good too.

My father gave me five shillings and my mother gave me her jade earrings, the ones I have wanted forever, and these made me feel almost rich.

"The earrings were to be yours after I am gone," Mamma said. "Lord knows your inheritance will be small enough, but you are growing up so fast, my Lydia! And even though everyone knows how I suffer from my nerves, the doctor assures me that I am unlikely to die for years. You had much better enjoy the earrings now while you are young and beautiful."

This afternoon I wanted to walk to Meryton, as with Father's shillings and my savings I finally have enough for the lavender gloves with gray pearl buttons in Savill's, but it rained and I am reduced to writing, which is even harder work than I expected and is making my hand ache. This evening, my aunt and uncle Philips come to dinner with the Lucases, if the rain does not cause them all to cancel. Lord, how I wish we lived in a town like them! It may be only a mile away, but it might as well be twenty. It is too dull, being stuck out here in the country.

I showed my journal to Mary, and asked if my mind was improved yet. She said that it was not.

"Just try to write one thing each day that is sensible," she said. "Or are you afraid someone will read it and discover you do have a brain after all?"

I grabbed the diary back from her.

"I am not afraid of anything," I told her. "But Mamma was right. I would much sooner you had given me ribbons."

THURSDAY, 5TH SEPTEMBER

*T*HREE MONTHS since I wrote in this diary, but *at last* something interesting has happened! I could hardly contain myself when we came back from Meryton, but skipped singing about the house until Father burst out of his office and shouted at me to be quiet.

"But it is so exciting!" I cried.

"Well, for heaven's sake, find another expression for your emotions. The racket!"

Jane suggested the diary instead. She said if I sat quietly to write, she would even do my share of this week's mending. It is not easy to sit still for so long, but I mean to try.

So.

Meryton has grown! Overnight, it has been transformed, from DULLEST TOWN IN THE WORLD to a positive DEN OF EXCITEMENT.

We had heard rumors, but at last it has happened! A militia regiment is come to Meryton and plans to winter here. We missed their entry into town (obviously—out here, we always miss everything), but Maria and Charlotte Lucas were there on errands for their mother and Maria ran all the way home to tell us.

Panting like an excited puppy, she burst into the drawing room where the others were reading and Kitty and I were playing with Napoleon. "Scarlet coats!" she cried. "Gold buttons and swords and all marching in time! One of them winked at me, I am quite certain of it! *Winked* at me! I nearly swooned!"

Lizzy raised one eyebrow the way she does that I wish I could imitate. Jane smiled, Kitty gaped, and Mary said she hoped Maria wasn't going to become silly because of a few uniforms.

"Don't be such a spoilsport!" I cried. "Maria, ignore her. Tell us *everything*!"

As Maria spoke, I could almost see the parade. The coats and the buttons and the bright eyes of the men, the proud horses of the officers, the pirouette of a young stallion, the crowds lining the street . . . Oh, I couldn't bear to be missing it!

"We have to go!" I ran to fetch my cloak.

Jane and Lizzy protested. *It's not proper . . . running to gawp at soldiers . . . we'll see them soon enough, I'm sure . . .*

I jammed my bonnet on my head.

"What a good thing, Lizzy, I traded that awful yellow ribbon

8

you gave me for the lilac," I cried as I ran from the house. "It matches my new gloves! How elegant the officers shall think me!"

They laughed and followed, just as I knew they would, but they could not catch me.

෨෧෨

We called on my aunt Philips when we arrived in Meryton. She rushed downstairs to greet us, skipping like a girl (which anyone who knows my aunt would agree was a fearsome sight—she has grown even fatter since the last time I saw her, and wobbles when she moves like one of Hill's legendary jellies).

"My dears!" She reached out to embrace us all at once, smothering us in powder and the scent of lavender water. "Isn't it thrilling? Isn't it grand? All winter! A whole regiment! Your uncle has already called on their colonel and invited him to dinner! In all my days I never saw such a body of men as their officers. Such fine athletic figures, such noble countenances! How much jollier our assembly balls shall be! How merry our evenings! Look through the window, girls. There are two of them now, walking past! Are not they the handsomest men you ever saw?"

Kitty rushed to the window. "*So* handsome," she cooed.

"Go, out to the street! You will see them better that way."

She pushed us out of the front door, gaily exhorting us to report on all we saw when we returned. I took Kitty's arm. Lizzy took Jane's. Mary went to the library to get some books.

"No talking, Lydia," Lizzy warned me. "No rushing up to unknown officers to introduce yourself."

"What *do* you take me for?" I responded.

Everything has changed in Meryton, *everything*! Townsmen walk taller to make up for their lack of uniform. Ladies look more elegant, and even the shops have perked up with the promise of more trade. Jane and Lizzy soon went back to my aunt's, but Kitty and I walked six times up and down the street. One of the younger officers, a shy-looking boy with sandy hair, blushed and nodded as we passed. His friend, a little older and darker, bowed and clicked his heels. I wanted to die then and there, but managed to contain myself until I was safely indoors.

"His face!" I howled. "The same color as his coat!"

"He was lovely though," Kitty sighed. "The way he tried to hide his blushing!"

"His friend was handsomer," I said. "The one who bowed. More . . . manly."

We laughed so hard Kitty had a coughing fit.

~~~

Mary just came in. She stood over my shoulder to read what I was writing and announced that she despaired.

"But Liddy is using your present at last!" Kitty told her. "Why aren't you pleased?"

"Mary does not approve of my choice of subject matter," I said without looking up.

"Parading before strange men!" Mary cried. "Going wild for a few scarlet coats! Is there really nothing else to write about?"

Jane came in to say good night, and tried to make peace as usual. "Those strange men have a purpose, Mary," she said. "There is a reason they wear that uniform. Remember, we are at war. If the French invade . . ."

"As if any of you thought for one minute today about the French!"

Jane murmured what an excellent thing it was to have Mary here to remind us (even though *she*, not Mary, is the one who brought up the war and the French). Mary, who is extremely conceited, agreed. Jane hugged her, and they both left smiling. Kitty finished brushing her hair and climbed into bed, but I stayed at my table.

My candle is almost out, or I could carry on writing all night. The things we saw today—the world will never be the same!

It is so much easier to write when you have something to write about.

FRIDAY, 6TH SEPTEMBER

*A*unt Philips came to spend the day with us, and so today we did not return to Meryton. I had hoped she would take us back with her in her carriage, but she stayed and stayed, and the fact that she talked of nothing but the regiment only made it more excruciating.

"The Colonel is a fine man—served in Spain! His face is badly scarred but it hardly matters, he is so noble and manly. The regiment is come from Derbyshire. Derbyshire, Sister! I have heard our brother's wife talk very fondly of that county, and indeed the officers are all most agreeable and gentlemanly. They are lodging in town. Some are married, and their wives—delightful creatures. Though it is not the *married* officers who interest us, eh, Sister?" She nudged Mamma and looked meaningfully at all of us.

"The lower ranks camp, of course," Aunt continued. "But they do not interest us either. The encampment is on the other side of town, a little out of the way by the river. The Colonel says we shall hardly know they are there, but I do confess . . ." She leaned in toward Mamma but whispered loud enough for us all to hear, "Soldiers, Sister! Remember the Atwood girl?"

"How could I forget?" Mamma gasped, rolling her eyes toward us. "Sister, do not speak of such things!"

"Who was the Atwood girl?" Kitty asked, and after a flurry of "My dears, I couldn't possibly say," Aunt *did* say, because she always does, and told us the story of poor Annie Atwood, a girl they once knew, who ran off with a soldier and was never spoken of again, not even by her own family.

"How do you *know* her family never spoke of her?" I asked. Aunt said it was common knowledge she never darkened their door again.

"It is a salutary tale, to be sure," she sighed, and then she and Mamma broke into giggles like a pair of girls.

I tried to ignore them, and thought instead of the camp. I imagine it smells something like the stables, all horses and dung and hay and sweat. There would be wood smoke, too, from the fires, and the smell of cooking, and bustle and shouting and noise. If I were a man, I wouldn't waste my time sitting about on sofas listening to Aunt Philips and Mamma giggle away about the past, and I wouldn't be like Father either, forever in his library, or like Uncle Philips or Maria's father, Sir William Lucas, lounging about indoors getting fat. I would live outside always, and have a splendid horse and gallop from one end of the country to the next, jumping hedges and fording rivers, and I would have a greatcoat with pockets full of useful things like knives and string, which I could wrap around myself at night when I slept under the stars, and I would have a gun across my back to catch the dinner I would roast over a fire, and have adventure after adventure, and one day when I had grandchildren their eyes would pop clean out of their heads with the excitement of listening to me.

As it is, being a girl, I can barely even ride.

"Lydia, are you quite well?" Mamma's voice brought me back to the drawing room.

"What did you say, Mamma?" I asked.

"You are quite flushed! Move away from the fire, child."

"Please may I be excused?"

I slipped out before Mamma could reply, and ran all the way to the Waire.

It is really only a small stream, but when I was a little girl I thought it a great river. There is a sort of beach by the bridge, where once when I was eight I tried to swim like the village boys do. I hid in a tree and spied on them for a week to understand how they floated, and one afternoon when they had gone I stripped down to my shift and waded in.

For a few seconds—maybe even a minute—it was marvelous. My toes curled in soft sand, my shift floated about my waist, and my whole body burned with cold. I lay on my back as I had seen the boys do, and water rushed over my head, and the world was full of bubbles, and it was absolutely splendid. Then the current swept me away and I nearly drowned.

A farmhand found me clinging to a rock in the middle of the water and carried me home, and it was all vastly dramatic. Mamma almost fainted at the sight of me, all wet and covered in mud and bleeding a bit, and Father actually smacked me. My sisters couldn't believe what I had done. They tried to make me promise I wouldn't do it again, but I refused. I said nothing in my life had ever been so wonderful, and I never admitted to a single soul how frightened I had been.

I still love the Waire, despite it trying to kill me. I haven't tried to swim again, but I do paddle sometimes, and I always go to it when I feel like I did today. Even though here it is only a stream, Mary says that about fifteen miles away it flows into the Lea, which flows into the Thames, which goes through London and then into the sea, and *that* must be quite something.

WEDNESDAY, 11TH SEPTEMBER

We have a new neighbor. His name is Mr. Bingley, and he is young, single, and rich—four or five thousand pounds a year, if my mother is to be believed. He is to rent Netherfield Park and will move in by the end of the month. Mamma is beside herself with the excitement of it.

"What a fine thing for our girls!" she cried, following my father into his library. Kitty and I crouched by the door.

"I suppose she will want him to marry Jane," Kitty said.

Mary announced that nothing good ever came from listening at doors.

"Papa will say he should be for Lizzy," I whispered to Kitty. "Seeing as she's his favorite."

"And then they will argue," Kitty agreed.

I had to put my hand over her mouth as we pressed our ears to the door, to stifle the sound of her coughing. Sure enough, Mamma and Father's argument was proceeding exactly as we knew it would.

"Lizzy is not a bit better than the others!" my mother protested. "She is not half so handsome as Jane, nor half so good-humored as Lydia."

"What about *me*?" Kitty glared at the door. "I'm handsome *and* good-tempered!"

I laughed, and jumped out of the way as she tried to kick me.

Mary sniffed.

"I suppose *you* think we are being frivolous," I said.

She plunged her nose into the book she was carrying.

"All this talk of husbands," she said. "When you could be improving—"

"Our minds, yes, I know." I sighed.

"She's coming!" Kitty hissed, and we scurried away across the vestibule.

The library door opened and our mother flounced out, calling for tea to soothe her nerves. She looked at us suspiciously as she passed and we all flew about pretending to be busy.

"You know nothing about him!" Mary hissed when Mamma was gone.

"We know he's rich," Kitty corrected. "And there is nothing frivolous about that."

Mary asked, Was that all she really cared for in a husband? Kitty said she hoped he would be handsome, too.

"I daresay you would sooner have a rector or a curate than a rich man," I teased Mary. "And spend your days tending his poultry and dairy, and listening to his sermons, and darning his socks, and be poor as a mouse."

Mary flushed. "Some of us may choose not to marry," she said.

"Not marry!" I cried. "What on earth would you do instead?"

"I should hate a poor husband," Kitty declared. "Jane can have her Mr. Bingley and his four or five thousand a year. My husband will have twice as much, and be so good-looking everyone will faint dead away as soon as they see him."

"Men like that don't marry girls like you, Kitty," Mary said.

"Girls like what?" Kitty pouted.

"Girls with no money."

"They do if they love them!" Kitty cried.

"Love!" Mary scoffed, but Kitty had seized the dress she was supposed to be mending and was dancing with it around the vestibule. "Rich!" she sang. "Handsome! Jealous!"

I laughed again and looked out of the window. The rain had stopped. Jane and Lizzy were walking together outside, doubtless whispering about our new neighbor. I don't know why everything always has to be about *them*, just because they are the oldest. Sometimes you would think my parents had only two daughters instead of five, but I'm sure we are all just as good as they are.

Kitty stopped dancing and threw herself onto the settle.

"What about you, Liddy?" she asked. "What sort of a man will you marry?"

Oh, rich and handsome, to be sure! That is what I was going to say. But the front door was standing open. Outside, Jane and Lizzy were walking toward the stream.

"Well?" Mary asked. "What sort of husband will yours be?"

I thought of the Waire winding lazily toward the sea, and the feeling I had the day the officers came to Meryton, that the world would never be the same. Suddenly rich and handsome did not seem enough.

"Someone magnificent," I said. "Who will make the rest of you wild with envy, and who will take me a long, long way from here."

WEDNESDAY, 16TH OCTOBER

Last night was the first assembly ball since the regiment came, and Aunt Philips was quite right—it was so much more jolly for their presence!

We met the officer who blushed when we passed him in the street. His name is Captain Carter. He is not as tall as I remembered him, and his hair is more ginger than sandy. His friend is Mr. Denny. *He* seemed *taller* than when first we saw him, and he has crooked teeth and bushy eyebrows, but they both cut a fine figure in their dress uniforms, and dance infinitely better than any of our neighbors, who look like farm boys next to them. They have another friend called Pratt, who has the biggest whiskers I have ever seen. I laughed when I saw them and told him whiskers were quite out of fashion, and he said, "Who cares, when I wear them with such *panache*?"

I am not entirely sure what *panache* is, but I like it.

I danced every dance. *Every single one.* My slippers are quite torn to shreds.

All the talk at home today is of Mr. Bingley, who came to the ball with his two sisters, one of their husbands, and a rich gentleman called Mr. Darcy, who is very tall, with flashing dark eyes and an expensive-looking coat. He didn't dance once but looked like he might die of boredom unless someone put him out of his misery and shot him first. The Bingley sisters (the Conceited Miss Caroline and the Hateful Mrs. Hurst) were dressed all in feathers and fans and held their noses so high in the air it was a wonder they didn't trip over their own silk petticoats. The husband was fat and had hair growing out of his ears. They are all ghastly, except for Mr. Bingley, who as well as being pleasingly rich is very beautiful, in a soft, brown-eyed sort of way, and has made himself exceedingly popular by promising to give a ball. He danced with Jane *twice*, which in Mamma's eyes makes them as good as married.

"He never paid such a compliment to any other lady in the room," Mamma informed Charlotte and Maria Lucas when they came to visit this afternoon.

"She still didn't dance as much as I did," I informed them.

Kitty giggled. Lizzy told us to be quiet. Mary rolled her eyes.

"Mr. Robinson asked whom he thought the prettiest woman in the room," Charlotte told us. "And he replied, the eldest Miss

Bennet beyond a doubt, there cannot be two opinions on that point." Mamma sighed happily.

"Every single dance," I said, but now they were all taken up with Lizzy, and with how she had overheard Mr. Darcy refuse to dance with her even when Mr. Bingley pressed him to, and how when Mr. Bingley said he thought Lizzy was pretty Mr. Darcy said she was only *tolerable*, which I think is hilarious because usually everyone thinks Lizzy is perfect, but Mamma is furious about, probably because he is richer than any person we have ever known and would be even more of a catch than Bingley, although she won't admit it. Well, let them talk! I danced more last night than any of them, and dancing is my favorite thing in the world.

THURSDAY, 14ᵀᴴ NOVEMBER

*T*oday we went to Netherfield. Jane has been there these past few days because . . . oh, it's a long story. I honestly think Mamma is a matchmaking genius. Even I am somewhat shocked at her methods, but I cannot deny that they work.

A few days ago, Mr. Bingley's sisters invited Jane for dinner, and Mamma wouldn't let her take the carriage but sent her on horseback instead because (Mamma said) she thought it was going to rain and that way the sisters would have to ask her to stay the night so she wouldn't get wet, and who knew what romance might unfold with Jane and the Beautiful Bingley under the same roof? Except that the rain started before Jane arrived,

23

and she got soaked through and caught a cold. She is too sick even to come home, and I doubt looks very romantic with her nose all red. Lizzy has been there since yesterday attending to her, and we went today to visit.

Netherfield is . . . like no place I have ever been, with a great long drive from the gatehouse, all bordered with lime trees, and meadows on either side full of the fluffiest sheep and fattest cows and glossiest horses. The house itself is all pillars and yellow stone and enormous windows, and double steps leading up to the biggest front door I have ever seen. Mamma was ecstatic. "Imagine Jane, mistress of all this!" she cried. "Oh, it will do very well for her, very well indeed! I can see her here plain as day!"

Kitty and I laughed, and she took offense. "This is important!" she cried. "It is Jane's future! It is all our futures!"

"Darling Mamma, we are only laughing because you are so happy." I kissed her, and she smiled again. That is the way it always is with Mamma. People mock her because she cannot hide her thoughts or feelings, but she has the best intentions.

The visit itself did not go well. Mamma likes to pretend that she is equal to anybody, but I could tell as soon as we stepped out of the carriage that she was nervous, what with the big house and *all our futures* at stake. The awful Caroline Bingley was there, and the horrible Mr. Darcy, who wouldn't dance with Lizzy at the ball. We went upstairs to see Jane, still streaming snot into her lace-trimmed pillows, and when we came back down to the drawing room Mamma could not stop talking about her to Bingley. *The greatest patience in the world . . . the sweetest temper I ever met with . . .* she babbled, and then straight into how lovely Netherfield was, as if she couldn't wait to move Jane in. I think, if Lizzy hadn't interrupted, she would have suggested Jane never come home at all, but marry him from her sickbed. But Lizzy *did* interrupt, and only made things worse, because then there was a whole conversation about which was better, town or country, and Mr. Darcy said how boring the country is compared to London. I must say, even though I have never been to London, I agree with Mr. Darcy. I *long* to go to London, but Mamma got offended again and said he didn't understand a thing, Caroline Bingley looked down her mighty nose at us, and Lizzy *defended* him.

Defended *Darcy*. Against her own mother! Who then lost her head and basically accused him of having no breeding. Bingley is nice and managed to keep a straight face, but his sister smirked, and Darcy looked thunderous. Lizzy actually winced, and diverted the conversation by asking after Charlotte Lucas.

I was thinking about the ball Mr. Bingley had promised, and what a very fine thing it would be, but he did not mention it once during our visit. In the end, I had to take matters into my own hands.

"Mr. Bingley!" I said as we were leaving. "Did you not promise to give a ball? It would be the most shameful thing in the world if you were not to keep your promise!"

Again Caroline Bingley raised her eyebrows, and again Lizzy looked mortified, but I think Mr. Bingley was vastly relieved to have something nice to talk about, and said that I should name the day!

Kitty was almost hysterical on the way home. "You were so forward!" she gasped between peals of laughter.

"I thought I did remarkably well," I said.

"You did indeed," Mamma said. "Remember, girls, when you want something, you must fight for it. Nobody else will do it for you."

For a moment, I did not recognize her. She looked so fierce. Then she caught us looking at her, and smiled, and kissed me. "A ball!" she cried. "What shall we all wear?"

Oh, yes, Mamma was quite right to send Jane on horseback, and I was right to ask for a ball, no matter how forward it was.

MONDAY, 18TH NOVEMBER

We have a houseguest! He is completely ridiculous but I don't think he is funny at all. In fact, I would like to murder him.

Mr. Collins—that is his name—looks exactly like a pig, with a big soft lump of a body and a nose like a turnip. Although he is a rector, I would not wish him even on Mary. He wears black from head to toe, with a white neckerchief to show off his dirty yellow teeth, and the only thing more awful than his greasy mouse-colored hair is the hideous round hat he insists on wearing whenever he ventures outside.

Mr. Collins is our cousin, and when Father dies he will inherit Longbourn, though we have never met him before in our life. Then, Mamma says, he will have the power to throw us out of our home and onto the streets without so much as a stick of furniture. "It is no use complaining," says Mamma (who complains about it all the time). "It is just the way it is. Men inherit, and women must hope for the best." Currently, Mr. Collins lives in Kent, in a parsonage belonging to a rich noblewoman called Lady Catherine de Bourgh. He appears to be quite in love and has a daughter Mamma already hates, because even though Mr. Collins says she is too sickly to have any proper accomplishments, she is extremely rich.

"*Lizzy* is extremely accomplished," Mamma said as Mr. Collins guzzled Hill's delicious lemon posset. "Why, she plays the piano better than anyone in Hertfordshire, and she is always with her nose in a book."

Kitty kicked me under the table. "Why is Mamma telling lies about Lizzy?" she whispered, and I shrugged to say I had no idea.

"Lizzy doesn't read half as much as me," Mary protested. "And she only reads in English. *I* am teaching myself Greek."

"Teaching yourself?" Mr. Collins looked appalled. "But what about your governess?"

"We don't have a governess," Mary said. "I have asked for one so many times, but Father says there is no point in educating girls . . ."

"We are not talking about you, Mary," Mamma interrupted. I caught Kitty's eye and giggled.

"*I'm* learning Greek," I minced beneath my breath. Kitty snorted. Mr. Collins turned his attention to me.

"And what does Miss Lydia read?" he asked.

"She doesn't." Mary glared at me. "She prefers chasing after officers."

I nearly choked on a dried fig. Mr. Collins looked confused.

"Lydia likes to be outside," Jane said, before I could respond.

Mr. Collins declared that outdoor pursuits were very admirable and even educational, but that I should not forsake books entirely. "For not reading will make you stupid."

"I'm afraid it is far too late for that," Father said.

Mr. Collins and Father both chuckled like it was the most amusing thing in the world. Jane squeezed my hand under the table.

"Monstrous, monstrous man!" I complained to Kitty when we went up to bed. "And ugly! So ugly!"

"You have to be nice to him," Kitty said. "Liddy, you have to try."

"Nice to him! Why? He wasn't nice to me!"

Kitty started on about Longbourn and the inheritance and being thrown on the streets, but I wasn't listening.

"I don't care if Mr. Collins stands to inherit half of Hertfordshire, I shan't be nice to him. I would rather beg on the street than ask for his protection! I would rather keep pigs!"

Kitty said nothing. I threw myself on my bed and began to write, jabbing my diary like my pencil was a dagger and the paper Mr. Collins's face.

"What are you doing?" Kitty asked after a while.

"I'm writing my journal. I'm going to make it as scurrilous

as possible. I mean to sell it when we're poor, and become a publishing scandal, and make us pots of money."

"Liddy, be serious. What will happen to us when Father dies?"

I put down my pencil. Kitty's face was soft in the candlelight, her eyes big and dark and frightened. It's easy to forget, sometimes, that she is older than me.

"Father isn't going to die for ages and ages," I told her. "I never saw a man in better health. But when he does . . ."

"What?"

"Well, we shall all have to go and live with Jane and the splendidly rich Mr. Bingley."

Kitty gave a snort of laughter and all was well again. But I can't help thinking, What if the future isn't Mr. Bingley and balls and dazzling husbands—what if the future is Mr. Collins?

I don't think I could bear that.

TUESDAY, 19TH NOVEMBER

The day did not start well. Mr. Collins insisted on accompanying us on our walk to town after breakfast. I thought I would *die* from the tedium of listening to him. Everything we passed compared badly to the grand de Bourgh estate— our bridge is smaller than Lady Catherine's bridge, our lanes are not so well kept, our very trees are not so tall.

"Though to be sure it is a pleasant county," he gabbled when Lizzy told him *we* were happy here.

We stopped on the bridge to watch a kingfisher hunting in the stream, and he seized the opportunity to educate us.

"What you see here, dear cousins," he said, "is a magnificent specimen of the female *Alcedo atthis*. The name is Latin, of course, but as Miss Mary would doubtless be aware it derives from the Greek *halcyon*. We know her to be of the fairer sex by the color of her lower mandible, which is of an orange-reddish hue, with a black tip. Is not that a fascinating fact, Miss Lydia?"

"Fascinating," I sighed as the kingfisher flew away.

No, the day did not start well and the mile to Meryton never felt so long, but within minutes of arriving nothing mattered anymore—nothing. For there outside the library was Denny returned from London. And standing beside him . . .

The gentleman standing with Denny was most *definitely* athletic. He has just joined the regiment, and is tall and strong but also slim and elegant in his dark riding coat, and when he took off his hat I saw that his hair was light brown and thick and just a little bit messy. He has a lovely smile, and a dimple in his left cheek, and his mouth is wide and generous—the mouth of someone who likes to laugh and eat and drink, and his eyes are a sort of golden hazel, and when he talks to you he makes you feel you are the most important person in the world.

Denny introduced us. I was last, as usual. That is what comes of being the youngest.

"Lydia." The handsome gentleman smiled. "I once sailed on a ship of that name, all across the Mediterranean."

"What were you doing on a ship?"

Lizzy said, "Lydia, don't ask questions!"

"I should like to see the Mediterranean above all things," I told him.

"Well, then you must," he said.

32

That was all, but it left me in a daze.

"Where *is* the Mediterranean?" I asked Mary when we came home.

She huffed and said she could not believe I didn't know, but Jane took pity on me and showed me on Father's globe. It is a very small sea, but it touches an awful lot of countries—France and Spain and Greece and about a hundred more I have never heard of.

The officer is coming to Aunt Philips's card party tomorrow evening. I don't know how I shall survive until then. I think I may die in my sleep—if I sleep at all, which is unlikely. It is past midnight and my eyes are no heavier than when I first saw him this afternoon. They are still too full of him. My pen is flying across the page.

His name is Lieutenant George Wickham.

WEDNESDAY, 20TH NOVEMBER

ather gave us the carriage, and we arrived early at Aunt Philips's. The officers were still dining with my uncle, while we ladies and Mr. Collins waited in the drawing room. Interminable wait! Mr. Collins talked incessantly, though I haven't a notion what about. Lizzy and Jane and my aunt murmured appropriate responses, while Mary read a book, Kitty played at solitaire, and I sat in unaccustomed silence upon the sofa, wondering that my heart did not leap out of my mouth at the slightest sound from beyond the doors. There were other ladies present, but I hardly know who—some of the officers' wives, I think. I wore my lightest spotted muslin (the very pale green with the pink trim), my arms and chest were bare, and yet still the room felt so hot I could not breathe.

He entered. His beauty in scarlet regimentals was overwhelming. The world went black and I thought perhaps I had died, but then Kitty nudged me and I realized that I was alive, but had merely closed my eyes. Still, I kept them closed a few seconds longer, the better to savor the anticipation of seeing him again. I thought, Surely he must be feeling it, too? For all the time my eyes remained shut, there was no one in that room but he and I. He approached the sofa. He seized my hand. I shuddered with delight as he confessed his most ardent and violent devotion.

"Lydia!" Kitty nudged me again, harder this time. I opened my eyes.

Wickham was talking to Lizzy.

Every woman in the room was watching him, but *he* had eyes only for my sister. Every ear strained to hear what compliments he paid her. Lizzy blushed—Lizzy, who never blushes! Everybody sighed—had he already professed his love? So soon? If he had, it was too vastly romantic! The air positively crackled with curiosity and excitement as the room held its breath to hear her adoring response.

"Indeed." Lizzy's voice rang out, clear and strong and not in the least bit amorous. "Sometimes when it rains the lanes become quite impassable for mud."

"Mud?" Kitty was outraged. Even Jane looked disappointed.

My aunt and uncle, Colonel Forster, and Mr. Collins sat down to whist. Two other officers and their wives formed another four. The rest of us crowded around the larger table for a game of lottery tickets.

Wickham and Lizzy sat together. I dashed to his other side. "I'll shuffle!" I squeaked, and seized the deck of cards.

"It is a silly game," Lizzy murmured to Wickham. "All chance and no skill, but the younger ones like it."

"You've never objected before," I muttered.

Lizzy's black eyes glinted. It was terrifying. I fumbled and dropped the deck. And then . . . "Allow me."

A scarlet-clad arm descended between us. A strong hand reached for the cards. Lizzy and I sat back like chastened children as well-shaped, nimble fingers gathered them up.

The cards danced as Wickham shuffled. He cut the deck and held it high in one hand, pouring them like a waterfall into the other. He fanned them out before him, swirled them over the baize, gathered them in equal piles, and flipped them expertly together before tapping them smartly on the table and handing them to me with a bow.

I sighed.

"A tip from a seasoned player, Miss Lydia," Wickham murmured in my ear. "There is nothing wrong with chance. The trick is knowing how to use it."

I stole a glance at Lizzy. Her eyes flickered from me to Wickham. For the first time in my life, I saw her look uncertain, and felt a surge of triumph. Wickham dealt, as elegantly as he had shuffled. I seized my cards and gasped.

"Is there a problem, Miss Lydia?" he asked.

"None whatsoever," I said. "I just appear to have rather a good hand."

Could he have . . . No, it was not possible . . . I looked at him suspiciously. He was calm itself. Could he have dealt me such a hand on purpose? He caught me watching, and winked. I could not stop myself—I winked back.

After that—of course—he talked with Lizzy all evening, all about Derbyshire where he grew up with Mr. Darcy, of all people. Even though, as we know, Mr. Darcy is monstrous wealthy, he has done Wickham a great wrong depriving him of some inheritance. It is vastly tragic for Wickham, but I don't see why Lizzy must monopolize him. I could be just as sympathetic if they would only let me. As it was, I had to make a great show of being interested only in the game, the fish I had won and the fish I had lost.

Thanks to Wickham, I won much more than I lost. "If we were playing for money instead of fish," I said, "I would be disgustingly rich."

Lizzy went pink and said not to be so vulgar, but Wickham roared with laughter, and it made me feel funny inside.

It is some consolation, I suppose, that I can make him laugh, though I wish he would take me seriously.

MONDAY, 25TH NOVEMBER

*I*t has rained continuously since my aunt Philips's card party, and the lanes, as Lizzy would say, are quite impassable for mud. The garden is become a swamp and may yet turn into a lake. Ducks have taken up residence on the lawn and yesterday Hill found a frog in the scullery. The trees have lost the last of their leaves, and the views from the windows are all gray skies and brown mud. It is the most dismal thing you ever saw, and yet here at Longbourn we are not at all despondent—far from it. We are tremendously cheerful.

A few days ago, Mr. Bingley and the Conceited Caroline braved the weather and the treacherous lanes to invite us all *in person* to the ball at Netherfield, but it was plain to anyone with half a brain he couldn't care a fig if none of us went except Jane. He gazed at her with big calf eyes for the entire visit, and she gazed back all pink and moony. They are perfectly adorable, their children will be perfectly adorable, their whole life together will be one happy bundle of perfect adorableness. I keep hugging her, and she keeps telling me not to be silly, but I can't help it. Love has made her more beautiful than ever—as if she has swallowed the sun. She is netting a new overskirt for the ball, but I don't suppose it will ever be ready, because every time she picks it up she puts it down again, sighs, and stares out of the window with a dreamy adorable smile.

That is the first reason we are so cheerful, and it is marvelous. The second is that Mr. Collins—*Mr. Collins!*—is pursuing Lizzy. Mamma is delighted. She says it is his way of making up for inheriting Longbourn, and it is the funniest thing in the world to watch them. *He* is all compliments and pleasantries. *She* cuts him whenever she can, and hides whenever she sees him coming. Yesterday afternoon, she braved the pouring rain and ran all the way to the farm to escape him, but even then there was no respite. "She is probably in the dairy," I told Mr. Collins when he inquired, and I nearly died as we watched him wade through mud and streaming manure to join her. She hid behind a bale of hay, and he got filthy dirty for nothing. He bored us to death all evening trying to save face by telling us how fascinated he is by cows, and Lizzy is still not speaking to me, but it was worth it.

I know exactly what I will be wearing to the ball. It is an old gown of Jane's, let down at the hem and out at the bust, but the prettiest white spotted muslin, with an embroidered bodice and sleeves like little puffed clouds. I shall wear white silk flowers in my hair, my jade earrings, and new dancing slippers after the last pair got ruined at the assembly ball. I shan't be as smart as Bingley's sisters or their friends, but I am sure I am an absolute *decade* younger than most of them. And anyway, I don't care about them. I don't even care about the officers—except for one . . . Maria Lucas has learned all the new dances from her London cousin, and is teaching them to us. Kitty and I practice all the time. I already have blisters on my feet, but I don't care. Mr. Collins has engaged Lizzy for the first two dances (she couldn't say no, after the cowshed) and has warned that he plans to monopolize her for the entire ball.

I am quite glad for once that I am the youngest and Mamma does not want *me* to marry Mr. Collins. It is so very difficult to resist Mamma when her mind is made up (like poor Jane riding to Netherfield in the rain), and marrying Mr. Collins must be one of the most disgusting things anyone could do. Poor Lizzy! I do feel sorry for her, but . . . and I know this isn't sisterly or kind or good . . . but with Mr. Collins pursuing *her*, Wickham will be mine all evening.

WEDNESDAY, 27TH NOVEMBER

*I*t is four o'clock in the morning. Kitty is snoring away beside me but I can't sleep. The ball—oh, the ball!

Wickham was not there. I have to write that straightaway. I looked everywhere for him the moment I arrived. Every scarlet coat made my heart skip a beat, but then I saw Denny and he said Wickham had been called away on business. Naturally, I was devastated, because the entire purpose of my evening was to dance with Wickham, and yet if I am honest I was also a little relieved, because Lizzy looked *really* beautiful last night—far, far nicer than I. I don't know how she does it—her dress was simpler than mine, and she had no flowers in her hair, and yet the way she carried herself, she looked like a queen, and made *me* feel like a common country girl. Even Mr. Darcy, who was so superior about her at the assembly ball, asked her to dance. It is much, much better that Wickham didn't see her like that. It can't be long now before Mr. Collins proposes. Mamma is quite convinced he will ask before he leaves, and Kitty says Lizzy cannot refuse, for if she accepts Mr. Collins and Jane marries Bingley, we shall all be doubly saved when Father dies. And once she is engaged, Wickham will immediately like me instead.

Every ball in the world should be like Netherfield. After last night, I don't think I can set foot in the Meryton assembly rooms again. The Meryton rooms are always so crowded, the floorboards so dark, the ceilings so low, there is never enough air. By the end of an evening we are all sweat and red faces and everybody panting like thirsty dogs. It was all very well before last night when I didn't know any better. But now the very idea of those evenings is intolerable, because Netherfield—ah, Netherfield is all sparkling chandeliers and mirrors and light! The ballroom floor is the color of honey, and even after hours of dancing the air was still sweet with the scent of lilies and roses. And the dresses! Such headdresses, such brightly colored silks, such gauzy muslins and delicate lace and expensive jewels! At first, I did feel ashamed of my poor old gown. But then the dancing began, and I forgot all about it, for I knew more people than anyone, and even though none of the officers are half as handsome as Wickham, I danced with every one of them, even Colonel Forster. So what that my dress once belonged to Jane, and that my hair was not pinned in the latest fashion like Caroline Bingley's, or my throat did not sparkle with fat diamonds like Mrs. Hurst's! I was infinitely more popular than they. And the supper! The pastries and jellies and creams, the ices and sweetmeats, the pies and fowls and meat cakes and wines and ales! The London ladies picked and pecked and watched appalled as I ate *everything*.

"I never saw a girl stuff herself so," gasped Hateful Hurst. "Why, she will never dance again!"

"They will have to roll her out of here," Conceited Caroline tittered.

But then the orchestra started up another jig, and the players were from London, so infinitely better than our local musicians, and off I went until the final dance.

How tired I am, suddenly! Perhaps I will sleep after all. Sleep, and dream of ball after glittering ball.

∾ LATER ∾

Mr. Collins has proposed to Lizzy! Kitty was in the breakfast room with them when Mamma made her leave, and she ran to fetch me to tell me it was starting. We tried to listen at the door, but Mamma shooed us away. Kitty, Mary, and I sat waiting on the stairs while Mamma paced the vestibule, and it was a bit like last summer, when the roan mare was having her foal, and everyone waited outside the stable to be the first to see it, except this time we weren't waiting to see an adorable baby animal, but for the promise of a roof over our heads.

The breakfast-room door opened. Lizzy came out first.

Mamma rushed forward to embrace her, but Lizzy pushed past without a word and rushed upstairs. I don't think she even noticed us all still sitting on the stairs. Mamma stepped into the breakfast room, already calling out congratulations to Mr. Collins, then hurried out again moments later and ran into Father's library. The bell rang. Hill was sent to fetch Lizzy, who walked past us and into the library with her jaw set and her eyes positively blazing.

We waited.

The library door flew open. Lizzy came out, smiling even though Mamma was scolding her. Mr. Collins stepped forward. Mamma tried to grab him with one hand while tugging with the other at Lizzy, who shrugged her off and swept back up the stairs to where Jane stood waiting on the landing.

"She has rejected him," Mary whispered in awe.

Mr. Collins went out for a walk. Kitty began to cry.

Mamma complained bitterly all morning. To Father when he ventured out of the library, to Jane and Kitty and Mary and me, to Hill, to Charlotte Lucas when she arrived to spend the day with us. Mamma alternately pleads with Lizzy and threatens her, painting a picture of what life will be like for us if Mr. Collins gets away.

"The inheritance!" she cries. "Longbourn! The workhouse, the streets, guaranteed poverty the moment your father dies!"

"I am not planning on dying *yet*," Father says, but Mamma ignores him.

"What will become of us, with such ungrateful daughters!"

Lizzy's hands shake as she busies herself with her stitching, and her neck is red, as always when her temper is up, but once when she thought no one was watching I saw her mouth curl into a smile.

It is evening now. Charlotte has gone home, and we are all gathered quietly in the drawing room. I am writing. Mamma, Jane, Lizzy, and Kitty are sewing, Father is reading the newspaper, and Mr. Collins sits before the fire pretending to look at a book, radiating gloom and offended pride. No one dares say a word. Every so often, Mamma heaves a reproachful sigh in Lizzy's direction and tries to look like someone starving to death in the gutter (a considerable challenge as she is almost as plump as Aunt Philips). Lizzy ignores her.

Mary just came in, looking even paler than usual, with her hair pulled back and wearing her best spectacles. She sat beside Mr. Collins and asked him what he was reading. He muttered that it was Saint Augustine, and Mary asked, Would he not read out loud to us?

We were all astonished, but Mr. Collins drew himself up like a drooping plant that has suddenly had a drink of water, and grasped his book more firmly.

"*The world is a book*," he announced. "*And those who do not travel read only one page.*"

On and on he goes. I cannot believe Mary is subjecting us to this. What point can there possibly be? I am glad Lizzy isn't marrying him, even if it means she wins Wickham. Lizzy and Mr. Collins! He is not just mean and ugly, he is so, so dull. How could I ever have wished it for her?! But then . . . what if no one else wants to marry us! Jane will soon be twenty-three. Before long it will be too late for her, and we are none of us as beautiful or amiable as her. Where *will* we live, when Father dies and Mr. Collins turns us out? *Is* it better to be poor than stuck forever with Mr. Collins? I don't want to live on the charity of others, and never have nice things or go anywhere and live always with my sisters . . .

No—one way or another, I will have the life I want. And in the meantime, I am not going to think about it.

THURSDAY, 28TH NOVEMBER

*M*r. Collins disappeared straight after breakfast on another long walk. The rest of us went into Meryton, where we found Wickham already returned from London, talking to Denny outside Savill's. He smiled gloriously at each of us as we approached, but then, after offering to walk us home, he spoke only with Lizzy. They walked together ahead of us, and I followed straight behind, glowering. Lizzy was wearing her new *noisette* pelisse, with rose pink gloves and bonnet. I wish I had asked for a pelisse, too, instead of my new red cloak. A close-fitting pelisse is so much more willowy and elegant. As we walked, I tried to carry myself as she does— very straight, with long, even steps and this way she has with her

47

arms, neither swinging them nor keeping them still. It is not as easy as it seems, and though I think I succeeded tolerably well, Wickham did not look at me once.

Maybe, if he had paid more attention to me and I hadn't been so irritated about Lizzy, I wouldn't have been so impatient with Mr. Collins when he returned for luncheon. I might even have felt sorry for him. As it is, I sat down in a foul temper, and all through the meal, as he droned endlessly on, all I could think was that it was *his* fault, because if he had not been so dreadful Lizzy might have accepted him, and then Wickham would be all mine.

When he is not boring us with the lives of saints, Mr. Collins continues to advise us on all matters farming, from Better Cow Husbandry to The Auspicious Sowing of Oats. Today's chosen topic was Hens and How to Improve Their Laying. Did we know how vastly improved the flavor of eggs was by feeding chickens exclusively on a diet of corn? There was nothing like corn to ensure a good yellow yolk! Did we grow corn, ourselves? Lady Catherine's hens indeed had no other diet. But then Lady Catherine's hens were an altogether superior breed of bird—why, their very coop is built of the finest ash by a French carpenter who used to be a duke before the Revolution forced him to flee Paris.

I shouldn't wonder if Lady Catherine's hens slept on silk cushions and produced solid gold droppings.

Lord, it was unbearable! I wanted to pull the cloth off the table, just to make him stop. I don't know how the others managed to stay so calm. They just sat there munching away as he wittered on, with only Mary showing the slightest bit of interest.

"Lady Catherine's hens must be very fine indeed," she said.

How could she? How could any of them listen to this man's babble? I don't care how much control he might have over us one day. No one should be allowed to be so dull.

If Jane had been herself, she would have restrained me. But Mr. Bingley went to London yesterday with no date given for his return, and Jane is of no use to anybody.

Someone had to say something.

"I should like to meet Lady Catherine's hens," I declared. "Truly, I cannot think which introduction I should like more— the lady or her chickens."

The others slowly returned to life. Jane dragged herself back from thoughts of Bingley. My father's lips twitched and even Lizzy smirked as I twisted my napkin round and round my fingers beneath the table to stop myself from bursting, and we all waited with bated breath for Mr. Collins's reaction.

He laid down his knife and fork. His cheeks still bulged with Hill's apple pudding, yet as he squared his shoulders and peered at us down his turnip nose, he was a picture of injured dignity.

"My dear cousin," he cried, spraying apple *compote* all around him. "Are you comparing Lady Catherine to a chicken?"

And I burst. Oh, it felt so good! I laughed and I laughed and

I laughed, until tears ran down my cheeks and Father ordered me to leave the table.

At the door, I dropped into a low curtsy. "Cluck, cluck!" I said.

"LYDIA!"

I ran.

Outside, the light was dying and the air smelled of wet leaves. Sparrows twittered in the laurel hedge and in the cow-shed across the track the milkmaid sang. I sat upon the big corner-stone with my back against the wall of the house and closed my eyes.

Skirts rustled beside me. I opened my eyes. Mary was standing in front of me. There were tear streaks on her face.

And at last I understood.

The reading last night. Saint Augustine. Her extraordinary new interest in chickens.

"No!" I cried. "Mary, you cannot be serious!"

She sighed and sat down next to me.

"If I marry Mr. Collins," she said, very slowly, as if she were speaking to a child, "we will all be safe."

"If you marry Mr. Collins," I replied in exactly the same tone, "you will be very unhappy."

Mary was silent.

"You can't marry him!" I exploded. "Mary, nobody should *ever* have to marry Mr. Collins! He's an abominable man!"

"He is not an abominable man," Mary said. "He is pompous

and self-important and not very handsome, but I believe he means well and—"

"Please do not talk about Longbourn and inheritance!"

"I love it here, Lydia," she whispered. "I know you cannot wait to get away, but I never want to leave. I love it all. This stone we are sitting on, the Waire, the trees, the farm . . . my little room and our good, solid furniture, my chair before the fire, my desk, my pianoforte, my books. The orchard in spring when the blossom comes, the autumn harvest, even the winter mud. To know that I should come back to live here, that it would one day belong to my children . . . If Mr. Collins is the price to keep it, then I assure you I am willing to pay."

For a while, I could only stare at her in astonishment. I have never heard Mary express so much emotion. I inched closer to her and took her hand. It is so pale compared to mine, and she is so very clever and bookish. It is a ghastly thought, but what if Mr. Collins *were* right for her? And what if I have made her lose him?

"I'm sorry," I said. "I didn't think."

"That's your trouble. You never do."

"I will apologize. I will tell him I'm mad—no, not mad. Then *he* will worry lest madness runs in the family. I will tell him I am immensely silly—that I am renowned for it—but that you are perfectly brilliant. I will tell him anything you want!"

But Mary said, very quietly, "I think you've done enough, Lydia."

She left. Jane, Lizzy, and Kitty came out, wrapped up against the cold. They called out to Mary as she walked toward them, and as she drew near Jane held out her arms. Together they headed toward the lane. As they reached the rise in the road, I saw the four of them silhouetted quite clearly against the sky.

"Wait for me!" I wanted to call, but they were already too far to hear.

SATURDAY, 30TH NOVEMBER

I dreamed of Wickham last night—a lovely dream, of the two of us playing cards together and laughing over our piles and piles of winnings. At some point in the early morning, I was conscious of the sound of horses, the carriage being brought round to drive Mr. Collins to the coach, but it was daylight when I stirred again, a beautiful morning, not like winter at all. Kitty opened the curtains and I woke to the feeling of sunlight warming my face through the glass. It was a while before I could rouse myself to get out of bed. It felt too good to lie daydreaming between the sheets. But rise I must, and did. Hill brought a jug of warm water and I splashed it everywhere as

I washed and then skipped downstairs to a hearty breakfast of toast and ham and eggs and marmalade and two cups of coffee.

I didn't apologize to Mr. Collins, and he didn't propose to Mary before he went, but "I've been thinking," I whispered to her while the others ate. "No one but you could be mad enough to want Mr. Collins. He will *never* marry. Then, when Father dies, you can stay and keep house for him."

"You are the one who is mad," Mary said.

"But isn't it the perfect solution?" I insisted, and she almost smiled as she admitted that it was.

Then Charlotte came. She and Lizzy went out for a walk. I began work on a new project, which is to re-trim every single one of my bonnets. It is slow work, but there will be precious else to do on damp winter days. Once I grew used to being still, I had a lovely afternoon. Today I worked on the little straw poke, which I am re-crowning with a scrap of pale blue satin from an old skirt of Mamma's. Napoleon snuck into the drawing room and curled up purring beside me, and despite the nice day we lit a fire, and everything was altogether cozy and pleasant and felt like nothing would ever go wrong again. But *then* Lizzy came back with a face like thunder, and before we could find out why, Charlotte's father arrived, all friendly and neighborly on the surface and per- fidious snake beneath, to tell us that *Mr. Collins is to marry his daughter.*

Charlotte! Maria's sister! That mousy, boring, plain old maid! Why, she must be nearly thirty! Charlotte Lucas, our friend, one day to be mistress of Longbourn! Stealing our cousin from under our noses when she must know we need him for ourselves! It was incredible. More—it was impossible.

"We shall all be cousins!" burbled Sir William. I thought that Mary was going to cry.

"Good Lord!" I exclaimed, to deflect attention from her. "Sir William, how can you tell such a story? Do not you know that Mr. Collins wants to marry Lizzy?"

Sir William went very pink and assured me that Mr. Collins was definitely marrying his daughter. Mary pulled herself together and picked up a book.

When he finally, *finally* left, I walked down to the stream. Lizzy was already standing on the bridge, throwing pebbles one by one into the water. I gathered some of my own and went to stand beside her.

For a while we both stood there, not talking. Without saying a word we began to compete, and it was like being children again, seeing who could throw the farthest, as if no time had passed and nothing had changed since those days when we all played together before some of us became grown-up.

But time *has* passed and things *have* changed and we do not talk of the same things now as we did before.

There is a small ledge low on the wall of the bridge. If I stand on it, I can lean right over and stare straight down at the stream. The winter waters are darker than summer, and faster, too, but there is a deep pool to the side where the water is dammed, near the beach where I tried to swim. I dropped my final stone into it and watched the ripples spread out.

"I cannot believe," Lizzy said, hurling her final stone, "that Charlotte will marry that man."

"I hope they have really ugly babies."

"Lydia!"

"Don't pretend you don't agree." I hesitated. "Did you know that Mary wanted to marry him? Do you think he would have asked her, if I hadn't made a fool of him?"

Lizzy joined me on the ledge and together we stared into the Waire.

"We both made a fool of him," she said. "Poor Mary."

"She didn't like him, you know. She just didn't want to lose Longbourn. And now Charlotte will live here instead."

"Well, I can't say *I* envy her," Lizzy said grimly. "Much as I love Longbourn, it seems a heavy price for anyone to pay."

"I shall put it all about Meryton that he only asked her because he could not have *you*," I grumbled.

"And what good will that do?"

"It will stop Sir William the Great giving himself airs." I grinned.

"You mustn't do that, Liddy. It isn't dignified."

It was cold and damp out by the water. We stepped down from the ledge and turned toward home. Lizzy pulled her pelisse closer. She looked so lovely—it seemed quite unfathomable to me that Mr. Collins should have moved on from her so fast to pick Charlotte. We reached the edge of the lower lawn, where everyone says you get the best view of Longbourn—the sweep of grass, the gravel drive, the soft gray house and the coppice of sycamores, the rosemary hedge Grandfather Bennet planted beneath the breakfast-room windows that smells so good in summer.

"Don't you regret it just a little?" I asked. "Refusing Mr. Collins?"

A slow, wicked smile spread across Lizzy's face.

"Not for a second," she replied. "I cannot imagine anything worse than marrying a man I don't respect."

"Or love," I added.

"Or love," she agreed.

"Especially when he looks like a pig."

"Lydia!"

I slipped my arm through hers. She did not pull away.

"Do you realize how often you all say that?" I asked.

"What?"

" 'Lydia'!"

"That is because you are impossible!" she laughed.

I would give everything—Wickham, the next ball, my new bonnet—just for the feeling of walking arm in arm across the lawn with Lizzy. I felt taller. More graceful. Prettier.

Equal.

Jane saw us from the breakfast-room window and waved as we approached. My heart bubbled over with love for her, too.

"Mr. Bingley will come back soon, won't he?" I asked. "And propose to Jane, and marry her, and make her stupendously rich?"

"Of course he will," she said lightly. "Who could resist Jane?"

"And then everything will be all right."

She actually squeezed my arm. "As long as we all take care of each other," she said, and together we stepped into the house.

TUESDAY, 17TH DECEMBER

*W*hat a strange day it has been.

It began badly, with a letter from Caroline Bingley saying that she and Mr. Bingley have settled in London now, and don't intend to return to Netherfield this winter. Jane read the letter and wilted. Later, Lizzy told us what it said. My mother wailed, Kitty sobbed, and Mary declared that it was only to be expected. Mr. Collins, who is staying with us *again* and driving us all to distraction, said how very sorry he was for us all and he wished everyone could be as happy as him and Charlotte. We ignored him.

"But you said Mr. Bingley would come back!" I told Lizzy. "*Who could resist Jane*, that is what you said!"

"Clearly, I was wrong."

"But I believed you!"

"Well, how was I to know!" Lizzy cried. "This is his vile sisters' doing, I am sure. I daresay we are simply not rich or grand enough for them."

My mother wailed even more when she heard that, and hurried to the library to give Father the news. Jane drooped past in her cloak and bonnet. Lizzy marched her out for a walk. Kitty and I sat on the settle, feeling helpless.

"Is this what rich people do?" Kitty whispered. "Take a house and install servants and footmen and horses and carriages, only to give it all up after a few weeks?"

"I wish I were a man," I said. "Instead of a girl, obliged to sit around waiting for no-good suitors to decide if I am fancy enough, or to throw myself at idiot clergymen. If I were a man, I could *do* something. I could become a soldier."

"But then you would have to go to war," Kitty said. "You would have to fight."

In the parlor, Mary started to thump out a funeral march on the pianoforte. Mamma, finding no comfort from Father, staggered toward the kitchen to seek consolation from Hill.

"I shouldn't mind fighting one bit," I said. "I imagine I'd be quite good at killing people."

"Well, *my* husband won't be like Mr. Collins *or* Mr. Bingley," Kitty decided. "*My* husband shan't have to rent a house like Netherfield, for he will have a dozen houses of his own. And he shan't disappear for weeks without a word either. He will be kind, and concerned only with making me happy, and he will adore me."

She screeched as Napoleon leaped suddenly onto the bench, a mouse twitching helplessly in his maw.

"Horrible beast!" she cried. "Make him go away!"

"Nevermore this winter!" Mamma lamented from the kitchen. "And we were all so sure that he would marry Jane!"

The funeral march turned into a dirge. The mouse squeaked helplessly. I ran outside before I started to scream.

If Bingley won't have Jane, I told myself, what hope is there for me? I am not half so beautiful, nor kind, nor good. Not even a curate will want me, let alone anyone of consequence, and then when Father dies and Charlotte and Mr. Collins turn me out, I shall have to sleep in ditches, and beg for food from kindly farmers, and probably die before I am twenty.

That is how I felt this morning when I ran out of the house.

Jane was on the big lawn, walking arm in arm with Lizzy. I started toward them. I wanted to say something to her—anything. I wanted to hug her, and then for her to tell me that everything would be all right.

But then I saw someone was riding down the lane. A scarlet coat—it was Wickham!

My heart turned a somersault.

He met Jane and Lizzy at the top of the drive. He dismounted and bowed, they curtsied, and then the three of them walked away along the lower path, with the horse following behind. They did not wait for me. Had they not seen me? I broke into a run to catch up with them, then slowed again—how vastly tragic would it be for them to turn and see me galloping across the lawn toward them! Away they walked toward the Waire, with Wickham leading his horse and Lizzy in the middle but slightly closer to him than to Jane. Again, I wondered how she does it . . . She never flirts—quite the opposite. She is always perfectly proper, and never raises her voice, and she never seems to make any special effort with her clothes but always looks so nice, even when she has been for a walk and is all windblown and muddy. She just smiles and says clever things and everyone is smitten.

I had to hear what they were talking about. They had disappeared behind the thicket that borders the lower path toward the paddock. Nobody knows this except me, but if you are prepared to get a little dirty, you can walk alongside the path through the thicket right to the end without being seen. I only hesitated for a moment. Then, after making sure nobody could see me, I ran lightly along the edge of the lawn and into the cover of the trees. Brambles scratched at my clothes and face. I pushed them away as quietly as I could, ducking and weaving my way through the undergrowth. A twig snapped beneath my shoe. I froze. No one seemed to hear.

Still hidden, I finally caught up with them as they drew level with the entrance to the paddock, when they were already turning back.

"A short visit," Wickham was saying. "I must hurry back, but the company at Longbourn is simply too pleasant to keep away."

My skirt caught and ripped on a low branch. Again, I froze. The others exchanged a few more pleasantries, then Jane and Lizzy walked back to the house. Wickham stayed behind, claiming he had to check something on his horse's saddle. I breathed again. They had not heard me.

"You can come out now, Miss Lydia."

My stomach lurched as the trees in the thicket began to rustle. I tried to crawl away. Above me, branches were parted and Wickham's head appeared.

"Miss Lydia," he said. "Oh, Miss Lydia."

He held the branches back for me. Blushing furiously, I crept out, ducking farther under his arm before stumbling onto the path, where I made sure to stand sideways from him so he would not see the rip in my skirt.

"You have mud on your face," he observed.

I rubbed my scarlet cheeks.

"And twigs in your hair."

I tried to smooth it. My bonnet was halfway down my back, hanging from twisted ribbons. Wickham said I was only making things worse.

"How did you know I was there?" I sulked.

"I'm a soldier. I am trained to detect spies."

"You've been a soldier for about six weeks," I objected.

"Well, you are not a very good spy." He laughed.

We walked together to the beginning of the path where it joins the drive, with the horse snorting behind us and occasionally nudging us to go faster. I wanted to smile and be clever like

Lizzy, but I couldn't think of a single thing to say. We went on to the main gates, where Wickham prepared to remount. I looked up the drive, to where Jane and Lizzy sat with their backs to us on the stone seat facing the house. Suddenly, I could bear it no longer.

"Do you like Lizzy very much?" I asked.

Wickham did not look offended, or even surprised by my question.

"She is very beautiful and agreeable," he said.

"And I just make you laugh," I said sourly.

Mary is right—I open my mouth without thinking, and words fly out. I blushed the hottest red I have ever felt, and stared at my feet, but when I looked up he was smiling—a teasing grin.

"I certainly cannot imagine Miss Elizabeth climbing through bushes to spy on people," he said. "You are quite unique in that respect."

I giggled and smacked his arm. He caught my hand, and <u>did not let it go</u>, but held it quite firmly, looking into my eyes as if he had something to tell me that was very important.

"I think that you and I could be great friends," he said, and then he let go of my hand, swung himself into the saddle, and trotted away. He turned when he reached the bend in the lane, and waved. It was all I could manage to wave back before he disappeared.

What does that mean? "You and I could be great friends"?

I don't want to be *friends*. I want him to be in love with me!

I was in such a rage of disappointment I could not return

to the house, but stormed off down the lane, and did not come home for hours. I was hot and even filthier when I returned. The others were all drinking tea. I threw myself on the sofa, declined refreshment, and glared into the fire. Friends, indeed! I thought.

Then little by little, I became sensible to what was taking place around me. In the far corner of the room, Mamma and Father were arguing—she insisting that he write to Mr. Bingley, he refusing. She began to cry. He sighed in exasperation and left the room and Mamma bit her lip to stop herself crying harder. Jane sat with Lizzy's arms about her, staring into the fire, a veritable picture of gloom, and Mary sighed heavily as she read, doubtless thinking of Mr. Collins, while Kitty frowned as she worked on a new bonnet with which she hopes to impress some officer or other.

Love, in our household at least, seems to cause an awful lot of misery.

When I was little, before someone decided it was wrong, I was friends with those village boys who used to swim in the Waire. We built dens together in the woods, and they showed me how to catch fish, and one of them—Thomas, he was the oldest— once made a fire to cook them on. The fish were burned to a cinder, but it was wonderful to sit swinging my legs on a tree stump, licking fishy charcoal off my hands.

Perhaps Wickham is right and friendship could be a splendid thing after all.

SUNDAY, 22ND DECEMBER

The day after I last wrote in this diary—the day after Wickham said what he did, about us becoming friends—we dined with him at Aunt Philips's, and he talked as usual almost exclusively to Lizzy, and I realized then that nothing had changed, nor would change, unless I did something about it. On the drive home, I pondered what it means to be friends with a person—and realized that I did not know. I am not sure I *have* friends. There is Maria Lucas, of course, and there are other neighbors, but in all honesty (and I think it is important at least to *try* to be honest), most of them (including Maria) could easily be replaced.

"You and I could be great friends," he said, but how did one go about making such a thing happen?

And then I thought again of those village boys, all those years ago, and I realized what it was that made us friends. It was the fact that we did things together—built shelters with logs and branches, climbed trees, caught fish. We would never have become friends just by sitting about chatting to each other in drawing rooms. I did not think Wickham would want to build shelters in the woods, but there were other things he could do . . . And so the following day, as we all prepared to walk back to Longbourn together after a visit to Savill's to buy a last few presents for Christmas, I pulled him aside and said, "Wickham, will you do something for me?"

"Anything you ask," he said, his eyes still on Lizzy walking ahead.

"Will you teach me to ride a horse?"

"To ride a horse?" *That* got his attention. "I must admit, Lydia, that is the last thing I expected. But do you not know how to ride already?"

"I know how to sit on a horse as it walks very slowly from one place to another," I said. "I want to learn to ride properly— to go fast, and gallop, and jump over things. Ladies do, you know," I added, in case he should think I was being very improper.

"I find most ladies are more concerned with balls and bonnets and practicing their accomplishments."

"Then you have a very narrow view of young ladies," I snapped. "I am very fond of balls and bonnets, but I should like to learn to ride as well. I don't think that is so very contradictory. I should also quite like to learn to shoot," I added, remembering my thoughts the day Aunt Philips came to bring news of the regiment when they first arrived, when I sat fidgeting upon the sofa thinking of all the things I would do if I were a man.

Wickham burst out laughing. Lizzy looked back curiously, but he offered *me* his arm, and together we planned when my lessons should take place.

And so I have ridden every afternoon for the past three days. Wickham is a surprisingly thorough teacher. I am learning in our paddock, on the mare he was loaned for his stay in Meryton. Her name is Bessie, and she is alarmingly tall, but also, he says, immensely docile and well trained, and perfect for teaching a lady.

"So, Lydia," he said, as he arrived for our very first lesson. "How serious are you about this?"

"Entirely serious," I replied.

"And you don't mind getting dirty? Doing tasks most ladies would consider unbecoming, or beneath them?"

"Not in the least!"

"Excellent reply!" And with that he led the mare to the stables, tied her to a ring, removed her bridle and saddle, gave me the bridle to hold, disappeared into the stables, and came out carrying our sidesaddle, with a brush and hoof pick on top.

"Lesson one," he said. "How to prepare and saddle your horse. Not the most elegant aspect of the sport, but something every true horseman or horsewoman ought to know how to do."

I did nothing else that day but brush Bessie from her mane to her fetlocks (I did not even know that horses *had* fetlocks), pick out her hooves, and put on her bridle and saddle, the task made all the harder by the cold, which numbed my fingers.

"I don't know a single lady who does this," I complained.

"Now you know how grooms and stable hands feel," Wickham said pitilessly.

On the second day, I prepared Bessie again, and then Wickham led me round the paddock, correcting the position of my hands, my legs, my back, and even my head as he taught me to stop, move on, turn left, right, change rein, and execute figures of eight, first at a walk, then at a gentle trot, as our breath made puffs of vapor in the air.

And then today, he put Bessie on something called a lunging rein and told me we were going to canter.

"But don't worry," he said. "You will be on the rein, and just going in a wide circle, so she cannot run away with you."

"I'm not worried," I said quickly.

He let out the rein. I squeezed Bessie's sides, as he had taught me. She walked forward. Wickham flicked his whip. She broke into a trot, throwing me about so my bones all rattled. Another flick and . . .

"I can't!" I squealed.

"Whoa . . ." Bessie slowed down. "What is the matter, Lydia? Don't tell me you are afraid! I thought you completely fearless!"

"It is so high up!"

"Then don't look down."

"I cannot help it!"

"Very well," he said, and took the reins from my hands.

"What are you doing? I don't want to stop!"

"You are not going to stop." He had tied a knot in the reins, and hung them to rest on Bessle's neck, well clear of her legs. "Now, Lydia," he said. "Do you trust me?"

"Why?"

"Do you?"

"I don't know!"

"I suppose that will have to do." He smiled. "Now I want you to hold on to the pommel—that is the front of the saddle—and remember everything I have taught you about your posture. Can you do that?"

"Yes," I said suspiciously.

"Good." He let the rein out again. "Oh, and I want you to close your eyes."

"What?"

"Trust me! I promise I won't let anything happen to you!"

And so I did as he said. I sat on Bessie, ramrod straight, chin up, heels down, my hands upon the pommel, *and my eyes tightly closed* as she walked, then trotted, then . . .

"Keep your eyes shut!" Wickham yelled.

I was flying . . . flying! With Bessie moving smoothly beneath me, and the wind rushing past, and the cold completely forgotten as Wickham whooped.

"Whoa!" he called again. Bessie slowed, and I opened my eyes.

"I did it!" I shouted.

"You'll make a horsewoman yet, Lydia Bennet!" Wickham grinned. "I knew you wouldn't be afraid for long."

Every bone in my body aches, the farmworkers think I am hilarious, my sisters think I am mad, and Mamma is convinced that I will break my neck, but I have done it! I have learned to ride fast!

"When can I jump and gallop?" I asked Wickham as together we removed the sidesaddle from Bessie.

"Soon."

"And shoot?"

"After the jumping and galloping."

He walked back to the house with me to take his leave of the others. Lizzy raised her eyebrows as we came in. "Goodness, Lydia, look at you! Spattered in mud from head to foot!"

But she was smiling as she said it, and as Wickham took a seat beside her and I dropped onto the sofa, she poured out wine and offered a plate of biscuits, and I thought how perfect it would be if life could always be like this.

"It was a good lesson today," Wickham told her. "Wasn't it, Lydia?"

"Monstrous good," I agreed.

In more ways than one, I realized, as I stood beside Lizzy,

waving good-bye as he rode away. For today I finally learned what it means to be great friends.

It means trusting someone so much you are prepared to do something terrifying with your eyes shut, knowing they won't ever let anything bad happen to you, and it is the best feeling in the world.

SUNDAY, 29TH DECEMBER

*I*t has been the best Christmas in the entire history of Christmases, better even than the one when I was little and we were given the doll's house, or the one when the spaniel's puppies were born.

The house has been full to bursting for days. Aunt and Uncle Gardiner came from London as usual with all four of their children, and from the minute they tumbled out of the carriage the place has been all noise and fun.

"We must gather holly!" William cried, as he always does.

"Ivy!" Philadelphia shouted.

"And rosemary and bay!" Sophy ordered.

"I want to paddle in the stream!" Henry yelled, but his mother said no.

And then we ran about the woods gathering greenery for Jane and Lizzy to make into wreaths, and raided the kitchen for mince pies behind Hill's back. Kitty and I have the two little Gardiner girls sleeping in our room on beds brought down from the attic, and the boys are in Father's dressing room. He pretends to mind, but secretly he likes to imagine they are the sons he never had (and who, life being so unfair, would have inherited Longbourn). "Good to have the house not overrun by females," he says, as he does every year, as William and Henry chase each other up and down stairs, and "That's the spirit!" as they thump each other with cricket bats.

Everything is topsy-turvy at Christmas—the house so full of greenery it looks like a forest, the tables and sideboards heaving with pies and puddings, sides of beef and gleaming hams, capons and carp and jellies and aspic, fires blazing in every room, so bright it is as if there were no night, mealtimes almost forgotten as visitors come and go. Some stuff their mouths and drink wine till they are red in the face and some fall asleep on the sofa. Others help to push back furniture so that we can dance to Mary or Lizzy or Aunt Gardiner at the piano, and Captain Carter on his violin.

Colonel Forster has married recently. His wife, Harriet, is about a century younger than him and very pretty. Kitty thinks her very fashionable, but her clothes are perfectly hideous. Tonight she was wearing yellow-spotted lilac with a double row of primrose ruffles at her skirt and neckline, and her hair pinned in so many curls she could not move her head. Wickham says she is trying to look older than she is, because her husband is so ancient—at least twenty years older than her.

"Do purple and yellow make a person look older?" I asked.

Wickham said no, they made a person look like a particularly dangerous mushroom, and made me snort with laughter.

There has been no riding since the Gardiners arrived, but I danced with Wickham a vastly jolly reel this evening, all whooping and clapping. He dances better than anybody.

"Look at the stars," he said when he left. "It will be a fine day tomorrow, Lydia. Shall I come back in the afternoon, and ask your mamma's permission to take you for a proper ride at last?"

"What, in the countryside? Do you mean outside the paddock?"

Wickham said that was exactly what he meant.

"I should like that more than anything!" I told him.

"Then consider it done. It will be my Christmas present to you."

He bowed, very formally, which made me laugh again, then moved away to take his leave of the others. He lingered over his good-byes to Lizzy, but I found I did not mind.

Tomorrow when we ride, I shall wear my new fur-lined gloves. I wish I could have a proper riding habit—I would make it red, with gold buttons, nicely fitted, with a gray necktie and a matching smart gray top hat. As it is, I will have to make do with my blue wool. Even so, I can see us now, galloping across the fields, jumping over ditches, the warm breath of the horses, the rising mist. How fine everyone will think us!

Yes, it has been the best Christmas ever.

MONDAY, 30TH DECEMBER

*E*verybody has gone. The Gardiners returned to London yesterday, taking Jane with them. In the past I would have complained at the unfairness of it. Lizzy and Jane go to town all the time, because they are Aunt Gardiner's favorites, but Kitty, Mary, and I have never been invited. For a moment, as they drove away, I felt desolate. I tried to tell myself that I couldn't care less about London now, when there is so much fun to be had in Hertfordshire, but as William and Henry and Philadelphia and Sophy climbed back into the carriage, you could almost see all the merriness and bustle and excitement and cheer being sucked in after them.

"Blessed peace!" Father said, but it didn't feel that way at all. It felt suddenly very quiet and cold and lonely.

We will keep the greenery and decorations up until Twelfth Night. Mamma is already planning the menu for our celebrations, but the extra candles are all out and the spare beds have already been put away. The Christmas pies are finished and it's to be a cold dinner tonight, so that the servants may rest.

Wickham was wrong about the weather. It has started to snow. We all ran out when it began, and played at catching flakes as we used to when we were children. But it was cold, and our boots and gloves and cloaks were soon wet—you feel these things more when you are grown up. We have put our steaming clothes to dry before the kitchen stove and our boots are stuffed with rags. I thought to walk to Meryton this afternoon to make up for the blessed peace at home, but Hill says I mustn't, in case the snow turns into a blizzard, in which case I might not be able to return. We are due at the Lucases tomorrow to celebrate New Year's Eve. Nobody was looking forward to it, but if the snow gets worse we may not be able to get there, and so now Mamma is desperate for us to go. She has told Father to order the farm boy to clear the whole road between here and Lucas Lodge. Father refuses. "It would be both unfair and impossible," he says, and so Mamma is sulking.

Everyone is bad-tempered.

"For heaven's sake, Lydia, stop fidgeting!" Lizzy cried as we sat sewing after luncheon. "If you are going to be like this as long as the snow lasts, I will strangle you."

"Couldn't you strangle her anyway?" Mary asked.

"That is a monstrous thing to say!" I cried.

"At least *I* am able to entertain myself quietly," Mary said. "*I* do not rely on the company of small children or officers to be happy. As long as I have my books . . ."

"You will die an old maid," I finished for her.

"LYDIA!"

I stormed up to my room, taking care to stomp on every single step along the way.

I paced up and down before my window all afternoon, but I never saw a soul. Wickham did not come, and I did not get my ride.

MONDAY, 6TH JANUARY

*I*t was a sorry Twelfth Night. Denny, Carter, and Pratt turned up out of the night, snow covered and red nosed, with wet boots from braving the roads on foot and breath smelling of the brandy they had drunk as they walked to keep warm. Wickham did not come.

"He had another engagement." Denny would not quite meet Lizzy's eye as he spoke.

"Where?" I asked.

Denny said it was not his place to tell.

"Why not?"

Lizzy said, "Lydia, go and tell Hill we're ready for tea."

"Did he send a message?"

"Lydia!"

I hate Lizzy when she's like that. And I hate Carter and Denny for all their mystery, and I hate this endless snow for keeping us trapped at home. It is not nearly so much fun without Wickham. Carter and Denny and Pratt are nice, but he is different. They do not let me win at cards, and when I suggested going outside to look at the stars, they said they had only just gotten warm. All they want to do is eat and drink and dance, but dancing is dull with so few people, and they don't dance nearly as well as him.

"Denny," I asked when we finally gave up on the dancing. "Will you teach me to shoot a gun?"

"Shoot a gun?" Denny's bushy eyebrows shot into his hair. Carter and Pratt laughed. "That is not a usual occupation for a young lady, Miss Lydia."

"No," I said. "I suppose it isn't."

Perhaps there has been an accident, and they think we are not strong enough to bear it. No, his friends would have been in a somber mood if that were so . . . Perhaps he has been sent away—maybe promoted into another regiment, and it is a great secret. But then surely he would have said good-bye?

Surely friends do not leave without saying good-bye?

The officers left early, when it began to snow again. Hill, who claims to know about these things, says that January will be bitter, and she wouldn't be surprised if it snowed for days. It can't—it mustn't! We have been snowed in at Longbourn before, when I was twelve. I remember the desolation of it, even at that age—the weeks of boredom after the first excitement, seeing no one, eating only potatoes and jam. We were fit to kill each other by the end.

Which would be worse: marrying Mr. Collins, or being stuck in a house with your sisters? Charlotte's wedding is on Thursday. Mamma says if we have to, we will walk through the snow to attend it, just to show that we don't care.

God! I already want to kill everybody *now*.

THURSDAY, 6TH FEBRUARY

*I*t did not snow for days, it snowed for weeks. I don't even want to think about it. We managed to avoid murdering each other, but it was a close thing on my part at times. Mary's music! Mamma's nerves! No visitors apart from the Lucases, who *unlike us* have a *sleigh*. No letters—no news of Wickham. Thank heavens for Kitty and Napoleon.

Anyway, it is all over at last. The air is warmer, we have had TWO WHOLE DAYS of sunshine, and the snow is finally melting. Soon the ground will be dry enough for riding again. Visitors will come to Longbourn, and Wickham and I can finally have our Christmas gallop. Though we have not heard from him for over a month, Sir Lucas (who has gone by sleigh to Meryton) assures us that he is still there, and I cannot wait to remind him of his promise. The lanes are still icy and treacherous and black with mud, but none of us cares a fig. There are new books at the library, Mary says, that she is desperate to read. There is fresh gossip to be had from Harriet Forster that Kitty is longing to hear. There is a fur tippet in Savill's I have had my eye on since before Christmas, which now, thanks to the money my aunt and uncle Gardiner have given me, I can finally afford.

Tomorrow, come rain or shine, we walk to Meryton.

FRIDAY, 7TH FEBRUARY

I was so happy this morning.

The weather couldn't have been better for our excursion. The sun shone brightly, and it was just possible, by skipping from side to side of the lane, to avoid the worst of the mud. Even Mary forsook her studies, donned her sturdiest boots, and set out with us to Meryton. I started to sing and for once nobody stopped me. Lizzy, Kitty, and Mary even joined in the chorus.

"We will rant and we'll roar like true British sailors,
We'll rant and we'll roar all on the salt sea.

Until we strike soundings in the channel of old England;
From Ushant to Scilly is thirty-five leagues."

That is how jolly we were on our walk—even my sisters were singing a sailor's song. The breeze came up but the sun stayed out. We were still laughing as we entered Meryton, cheeks flushed, skirts and hair swept by the wind. Kitty dared me to sing another verse as we walked down the street, but Lizzy forbade it.

Mary went straight to the library. Lizzy and Kitty and I spilled into Savill's.

"It's still here!" I cried, rushing to the glass case where the tippet lay in all its glorious, honey-furred splendor. "And I have just enough money!".

And then we saw him.

Wickham, standing with his back to us at the end of the counter, every bit as dashing as ever with a dark cloak thrown over his red coat.

"Wickham!" I cried. "We are here at last!" He did not turn. As I started toward him, I glanced at what he was holding.

"Good God!" I said to my sisters.

Lizzy followed the direction of my gaze.

"Goodness," she said.

It was a hatbox. Huge, pink and black, with matching ribbons.

"Wickham?" I called.

At last, he turned. For the ghost of a moment, he held my

eye, but he immediately turned away. Something caught in my throat—what could be the meaning of this?

A girl was standing at the other end of the counter. Scrawny, red-haired, and freckled, about the size of a shrimp, accompanied by an older lady. She called him to her.

"It is Mary King," Kitty murmured. "And her companion, Mrs. Roberts."

"Wickham!" I repeated, louder this time. I waved, sending a pile of glove boxes crashing to the floor. Everyone turned to stare. Mr. Savill huffed. I scrambled about the floor, attempting to pick up the gloves. Wickham could not ignore that . . . Excusing himself for a moment, he stepped toward us, still carrying his ludicrous box.

He bowed. "Miss Elizabeth, Miss Kitty, Miss Lydia."

"The snow's melted!" I informed him, hot with embarrassment as Lizzy pulled me up. "When shall we have our Christmas gallop?"

"Lydia!" Lizzy nudged me.

"What? He promised!"

"Hush," she said, with a meaningful nod as Miss King and Mrs. Roberts were approaching.

Kitty and I exchanged astonished glances. More curtsies, and then Mrs. Roberts inquired, how long had we been snow-bound at Longbourn, and how *did* we manage, so isolated out there? Lizzy said we tolerated it as best we could. And in summer, so close to the water—the gnats! Lizzy said we tolerated those, too. And then the Shrimp sighed and said please could they go, for there was nothing in Savill's to her liking, and the shop door gave a great tinkle as they all left.

I understood then, about the hatbox.

He was carrying her shopping!

∾⌇∽

It was my Aunt Philips who told us about Miss King's ten thousand pounds. "She had it from her grandfather," she told us when we called on her. "And Wickham, who as you know is without a penny, has been like a bee to a honeypot ever since. Oh, my dears! I wanted to come to Longbourn to tell you, but the snow! It has been all the talk of the town. A most imprudent match for her, but then, he is so very handsome!"

Lizzy said, "Thank you, Aunt, we had better be off."

Kitty cried most of the way home.

"Nobody will marry us," she wailed between sobs. "We will all grow to be old maids like Mary, and our only companions will be cats."

"There is nothing wrong with cats, unless they are like Napoleon," Mary observed. "And what does Wickham pursuing Miss King have to do with us?"

"We all thought he liked Lizzy!"

"Yes, but not really," Lizzy said calmly.

"Don't you *mind*?" I cried.

"I only mind if people think I care. Oh, stop looking at me like that! Wickham is very handsome and agreeable, but he is not the sort you *marry*! He is for . . . amusing conversations, and

88

making you feel pretty. It is very different altogether. People can't marry where there is no money—it is not sensible. I know it makes you wild, Lydia, but it is just the way of the world. You must have known it could not last forever."

"But he betrayed us!" I told her. "Didn't you see, in Savill's? He *cut* us. All those times he came to Longbourn, all that talking and dancing, yet he barely spoke to us. Are we not good enough for him now?"

Lizzy is right. In my heart, I always did know it could not last forever—that Wickham could not keep coming to our house, that with no money on either side he could not marry Lizzy. But where did that leave me?

What of friendship, I would like to know?

I don't know how Lizzy can be so calm. We were just coming to the bridge. I picked up the largest stone I could find, and hurled it into the water.

MONDAY, 10TH FEBRUARY

I burned my candle late into the night going over this diary, and the memory of what I read still mortifies me.

I thought he was my friend, but he is no different from the rest. He is no different from Mr. Bingley, who thinks we are not rich enough, or Mr. Darcy, wincing at Mamma at Netherfield, curling his lip when I asked about the ball. Wickham is embarrassed to be seen with us—he doesn't think we are good enough either.

It's early, but I am already awake, and I am in a rage. I hate Miss King and her stupid ten thousand pounds! Why could *I* not have ten thousand pounds? I'm sure I deserve them infinitely more than she does. If I had ten thousand pounds I would go straight out and buy a house with no entailment for stupid male cousins, with my own horses to ride and a fine carriage so I never had to walk through muddy lanes to Meryton again, and everyone would think I was marvelous because I would let my sisters live there, too, while I went about the world having adventures that people would write about in the papers. What will Miss King do, but marry Wickham and gawp at him and buy more and more hats?

"I think that you and I can be great friends," he said.

Fool, _fool_, FOOL! We were _never_ friends.

I am going to burn this diary. It is too mortifying. What if years from now somebody reads it, when I am old or dead or languishing in the poorhouse? How they will jeer at me! Or worse . . . what if they read it NOW? My sisters! While I am still alive! _Here_, living under the same roof, quite close enough to hear their sides split as they roar with laughter, because I was stupid enough to believe that Wickham liked me.

I did not know it was possible to feel so disappointed in a person.

But if Wickham thinks I am going to lie mooning about just because he is trotting around town carrying a freckled heiress's hatboxes, then he doesn't know Lydia Bennet.

THURSDAY, 30TH APRIL

*W*ell, I did not burn the diary—I just shoved it out of sight beneath my mattress and forgot all about it. Hill found it this morning when she decided to turn all the mattresses for airing, and I suppose I may as well write as not.

Life carries on much as it did before Wickham abandoned us for Miss King. Thank goodness the other officers are not so fickle. We walk into town, we visit Savill's or the library (which has become quite the meeting place since they have taken to serving tea there). Meryton is very elegant these days, and I am glad for all my re-trimmed bonnets. I have embarked on a new exercise for spring, the Revival of Ancient Cloaks. I have found an old one of Mamma's, parrot green. She was going to give it to the poor, but I rescued it from the basket. I have cut it down to a short and swishy cape, added an ivory satin collar, and am trimming it all round with ribbon of the same color. It will be quite the smartest thing you ever saw when it is finished, and I cannot wait to show it off. At the library, we drink tea and chat (Mary says flirt) with whomever is about. There is always someone, and it is all tremen- dously gay. I have bought a coral bracelet, which will look very well with the green cape. I wanted the necklace, but did not have enough. Then when the library closes, we step across the street to Aunt Philips's, or we call on Mrs. Forster. I am great friends with her now. It makes Kitty cross, because she says she was Harriet's friend first, but she is always ready for a party or a dance or a game of cards. And then there is dinner, and cards, or we push the furniture back for dancing, and we eat and drink some more. We return late in Uncle's carriage, or sometimes we even stop at his house for the night, and don't come home at all. It is all very merry and jolly, and all the more so since Lizzy left. She went into Kent last month to visit Charlotte-the-Husband- Stealer-Collins and the Pig-Faced Clergyman. I am glad she is gone—she only nagged when she was here. "Must you go out *again*, Lydia?"—"Can you not talk of anything other than uniforms?"—"Mamma, you must tell Lydia to be sensible!" I love Lizzy, I really do, but ever since Wickham deserted us, she is become boringly grown-up.

Of Wickham himself, there is little sign. Miss King the Great Heiress does not attend parties with officers, or dance or drink wine or play cards. Miss King visits a close circle of family friends where doubtless she executes impeccable concertos on the pianoforte, and warbles a few polite songs chosen for her by Mrs. Roberts before retiring early to bed. Wickham, I am told, trots about her like a well-trained lapdog, panting for his ten-thousand-pound reward. When our paths do happen to cross, in the library, in a shop, in the street, I am careful to show him how little I care about his defection. I laugh—God, how I laugh! The first time it happened, I was walking with Carter, who nearly jumped out of his skin with the honk I made! Lord knows what he thought of me, but I don't really care. He laughed back, that was the main thing, and I am sure that Wickham noticed.

I am the most carefree girl in England.

SUNDAY, 10ᵀᴴ MAY

*J*t is all changed again.

Firstly, Miss King is gone to Liverpool, to stay with her uncle! Aunt Philips says she was discovered walking alone along the Waire with Wickham, close to the soldiers' camp. Mrs. Roberts wrote to the uncle to ask what she should do, and he wrote back to say she was to go North immediately. And quite right, too, says Aunt, forgetting how much she enjoyed gossiping about them before. "A young lady like her, carrying on so with the likes of Wickham!" I did feel a little sorry for Miss King when she told us. Banishment to Liverpool seems a very big punishment for a little walk, and why does no one talk of punishing Wickham?

"How long will she be away?" Kitty asked.

"Oh, indefinitely!" Aunt replied. "For there are prospects for her up there. Good prospects, with the son of her uncle's business partner."

"How does Wickham bear it?" Kitty is so gullible. I think she honestly believes Wickham was fond of Miss King.

"Poorly, I should think," Aunt replied. "For there are few prospects left for him here."

He joined us this evening—strolled into Harriet Forster's drawing room for the first time in months, as tranquil, jolly, and handsome as ever. "Miss Lydia," he said with a smile. "I believe I owe you a ride in the country."

"Mr. Wickham," I replied coldly. "I am sorry to hear your financial interests have gone north."

"Lydia?" He looked at me closely. "Are you angry with me?"

"As if I cared enough to be angry!"

"I have upset you," he said gravely.

"No! Yes . . ." I gave up. "Wickham, you *dropped* us! For *Miss King*. Lizzy says you pursued her because she is rich, and that it is the way of the world, but we were *friends*."

"I am sorry."

I looked up at him. He stood with his head bowed and hands clasped, and did appear truly contrite. "I had . . . I did not . . . Lydia, would it help to know that it was Miss King who pursued *me*?"

"Surely you do not expect me to believe that?" I cried. "Why would she do that?"

"Am I not pleasing enough?" Wickham looked offended.

Yes, I do despise myself. Yes, I do still feel sorry for Miss King, and yes, I wish I were not so easily bought. But oh, I do so want that gallop! I did try to remain aloof as we sat down to play, but I caught his eye as he dealt, then looked at my cards—once again, his magic had given me a winning hand. And then there was dancing, and a jolly reel with him about the room, and I had forgotten how much I like to dance with him.

How we laughed tonight! Harriet devised the idea of dressing one of the officers in women's clothes, and sent me to my aunt's to fetch a gown to fit him. I ran all the way there, nearly knocking over Aunt's friend Mrs. Perry as I went. "One of those wild Bennet girls," I heard her tell her companion as I ran on. Harriet says Wickham is a scoundrel, but what has he done, really? Miss King is rich and ugly, and he is handsome and poor. It is just the way of the world, as Lizzy would say. I wonder what *she* will think when she hears the news. Even if Wickham is "not the sort you marry," she must be pleased. I am going to write to tell her—no, it is only a week until she returns. I am going to wait, and tell her to her face. How happy it will make her, and what a jolly spring and summer we shall have now that we are all friends again!

That is what I was thinking as I scribbled away happily in bed. Then I became aware of Kitty sniffling beside me, and put down my pencil to ask what was the matter.

"They're leaving!" Kitty sobbed. "The whole regiment! Harriet told me tonight. They are leaving by the end of the month for their summer quarters in Brighton! Harriet says they may never return."

Leaving? The whole regiment?

"Surely you are mistaken," I said. "Surely Wickham . . . one of them would have said something. Why did no one say anything?"

"Only the Colonel and Harriet know. He received the orders today, and is to tell the men tomorrow. I asked Harriet if I could go with her, and she said she would speak to the Colonel." Kitty was coughing now, the way she always does after crying. "But what if he says no?"

Kitty, go to Brighton, and not me? I could not let that happen!

"Maria's cousin went to Brighton last year," she sniffed. "Do you remember?"

"We should all go!" I said. "We should tell Father we want to go for the summer. We'll say it's for your cough. Seawater is the best thing for coughs—everyone knows that. Mamma will back us up."

"But will Father agree?"

"He'll have to." I lay on my back, staring at the ceiling. "Just think, Kitty. Us, in Brighton! Sea-bathing, and walking along the beach."

"Maria's cousin said . . . the dearest little shops . . ." Kitty was beginning to drift into sleep, still coughing gently. "And monstrous smart assemblies . . ."

I will catch Mamma as she is dressing in the morning, and

make her speak to Father straight after breakfast. He is always most amiable when he has eaten. Brighton! I shan't tell Wickham we are going. What a surprise that will be! We shall have a chance meeting, on a cliff, or perhaps a beach, or at a ball . . . Yes, a ball, so that we can dance. We shall have a chance meeting, and he will say, "Why, Miss Lydia, how well the sea air becomes you," and perhaps we will go for that ride at last. We will gallop along the beach!

How wonderful life is. Kitty's coughs have turned to snores. I am going to sleep now, too.

SUNDAY, 17ᵀᴴ MAY

*F*ather said no, of course, despite Mamma pressing and
me begging and Kitty coughing a great deal. He said,
Why should he go to such vast expense to entertain us,
when all *he* wants is to stay at home? If we want to bathe, there is
always the Waire.

"The Waire?" Mamma cried. "But Lydia nearly drowned in
it when she was a child!"

"Yes, and it is such a little stream," Father agreed. "Imagine
the damage she could do herself in the English Channel."

"But in Brighton there are attendants . . . the swimming is
supervised . . . there is no risk to anyone!"

Father said he would not change his mind, but Mamma has not given up.

Lizzy and Jane are no help at all. They came home a few days ago, and were utterly unsympathetic to our cause. Kitty and I went to meet their coach in the hope of engaging their help for the Brighton project before they saw Father. I was so looking forward to seeing them—especially Lizzy, to tell her about Miss King—but they showed not the slightest interest, not either in the officers leaving, or our plans for a Brighton summer, or even in Miss King being sent away from Meryton.

"Wickham is safe!" I told Lizzy.

"And Mary King is safe," she corrected, in her new boring, sensible way.

Lizzy has a secret, and I have found it out.

It wasn't difficult. Jane and Lizzy think when they go to their room and close the door that nobody can hear them, but we can. Our bedrooms used to be one big room, which has been divided by building closets in the middle of it. The closets are made of wood, and there is a small crack in the back of ours. If you climb in and put your ear to it, you can hear *very clearly indeed*.

The secret is this. Mr. Darcy has proposed to Lizzy! *Mr. Darcy!* After all his ignoring her at balls, and sneering at Mamma, and looking down his nose at the rest of us! She has refused him, just as she refused Mr. Collins, and quite right, too. Lizzy said that when he proposed to her, he made it very clear he did not think her family was good enough for his—that he was doing her a great favor in proposing, the proud, horrible man! But—he has ten thousand a year! And even though Lizzy took great pains to say how much she despised him, if Wickham is the sort of man one doesn't marry because he is poor, surely that makes Mr. Darcy the sort of man one doesn't refuse because he is rich?

Could she do that—could she actually marry him for that reason?

There is another secret, too, which is much more horrible.

Last summer, Wickham tried to elope with Mr. Darcy's sister, who is called Georgiana and is the same age as me. Mr. Darcy wrote a letter to Lizzy to explain, and Lizzy read it out to Jane. Georgiana was at Ramsgate with her companion, and Wickham was there too, and he convinced her to run away with him. He planned everything and they were almost on their way when Mr. Darcy turned up and put an end to it all.

"She was persuaded to believe herself in love." That is what Mr. Darcy wrote to Lizzy.

Wickham almost destroyed Georgiana. She was so in love with him she was prepared to risk everything—her reputation, her fortune, her connection to her family—just to run away with him, but as soon as he found out that Mr. Darcy would not let him see a penny of her money, he disappeared, and left her brokenhearted.

I never thought that he could be so unkind.

And now I am mortified again . . . Yesterday, in the coach

coming home—how I went on! Wickham this, Wickham that! Silly little Lydia, always running after Wickham, convinced that he is her friend, even though he did not speak to her for months, even though he abandoned her for a wealthy, freckled shrimp he didn't even like! I don't believe for a minute that he didn't pursue Miss King, and what he did to Georgiana Darcy was wrong. Lizzy watches me now all the time—what a fool she must think me, falling again and again for his charm and lies . . . I have to get away. I have to leave Meryton, where they all think me foolish and stupid. Oh, they are so superior! I swear that if I stay I will die—killed by their sniffs and frowns and the eyes they roll behind my back when they think I cannot see! But where can I go? There is nowhere! *Nowhere!*

I have to think of something.

SUNDAY, 24TH MAY

*B*righton. That is where I am going.

I spent a great deal of time with Harriet Forster this past week. Kitty's cough has not gone away, and Mamma has not allowed her outside. On Wednesday, I went alone to the library with Mary. I did not mean to do what I did. I swear on Napoleon's life that when we set out for Meryton, I thought only to distract myself by taking tea with whoever happened to be there. It is not my fault that that person was Harriet Forster.

We chatted and drank tea. The following day, we went shopping together for hats, and the day after we spent the afternoon cozily embroidering dancing slippers in her private drawing room. And then yesterday we took tea together again at the library.

"What a delightful few days these have been." She sighed. "How sad I shall be to see them end when we go to Brighton!"

I didn't do it on purpose. Not entirely, anyway.

Did I think, Harriet asked, that Kitty's health would benefit from some sea air?

It was just one of those moments when it feels like time has stopped, and you know that what you say next is going to change everything.

"Alas," I said, very carefully. "Kitty's health is vastly fragile, and Mamma will not let her out of her sight."

I did not say more than that. I did not need to.

Harriet invited me to Brighton there and then, with never another thought for poor Kitty.

Lizzy is doing all she can to try and stop me going. I have heard her actually begging Father to forbid it. "Vain, ignorant, idle, and absolutely uncontrolled"—those were her actual words about me, and when I heard them I honestly felt like a dagger was being twisted in my heart.

Is that really what she thinks of me? Or is it what *Mr. Darcy* thinks? Even though she has refused him, is she seeing me now through his eyes? Does she wish she had not refused him? I have kept her secret so carefully, knowing how Mamma would react if she knew Lizzy had turned down such a match—and she says all this?

I wasn't sure, when Harriet first issued her invitation, that I wanted to go, on account of Wickham also being there. I have been very cold toward him since I heard the secret about

Georgiana Darcy. I have not danced with him once, or allowed him to deal my cards, and I have made a very clear point of favoring all the other officers in Meryton over him, and when he has come to dinner—Mamma still invites him, and I cannot very well say why she should not—I have always sat right at the other end of the table. In truth, if I am to go away, I would rather be anywhere that he is not. But Lizzy saying those things—oh, I will go to Brighton, if it is the last thing I do, and I will show her what I am capable of! I shall bathe in the sea, and I shall make whole rafts of elegant new acquaintances, and I shall probably come back with a husband—I would come back with *two* if I could, just to prove that I am as capable as she is of getting proposals! And I am not going to allow an insignificant matter like *Wickham* being there to stop me.

Father told Lizzy there would be no peace in this house until he agreed to let me go, and he was right. There wasn't. And now I am off.

"But Harriet was to ask *me*!" Kitty wailed when Father said I could go. "She was my friend first!"

Mary, who was in the library when Harriet asked me and heard every word of our conversation, says there is a special place in Hell for girls who betray their sisters, and that I am heading straight for it, but I am not going to think about that now.

"Mamma says you have to fight for what you want," I told her.

Mary said, "Not if it means trampling all over other people to get it," but she doesn't understand a thing.

Harriet has told me everything we shall do—though she has

never been to Brighton, she has been to Weymouth, and so she knows all about the seaside. We shall bathe every day, and go on excursions, and there will be boating parties, and I will learn to sail, and everyone will be amazed at how naturally nautical I am.

I may be going to Hell, but I am going to Brighton first.

Brighton

ORIGINALLY A FISHING VILLAGE ON THE SOUTH COAST,
IT BECAME A HEALTH SPA IN 17-SOMETHING-OR-OTHER
WHEN DR. RUSSELL DISCOVERED THE BENEFICIAL EFFECTS OF
DRINKING AND BATHING IN SEAWATER.

NOW A SPARKLING RESORT,
PATRONIZED BY THE PRINCE OF WALES HIMSELF!
THE OPPOSITE OF HERTFORDSHIRE!
AND FROM TOMORROW, THE RESIDENCE OF
MISS LYDIA BENNET.

BRIGHTON
FRIDAY, 5TH JUNE

MY DEAR FAMILY,

HERE I AM, SAFELY ARRIVED IN BRIGHTON, AND IT IS EVERY BIT
AS DELIGHTFUL AS I EXPECTED. IT IS A CHARMING COLLECTION
OF QUAINT FISHERMEN'S COTTAGES AND ELEGANT NEW
BUILDINGS, ALL WHITE TRIM AND BOW WINDOWS, QUITE THE
SMARTEST I HAVE EVER SEEN. WE ARE LODGED VERY NEAR THE
SEA AND CLOSE TO GLORIOUS SHOPS THAT PUT POOR SAVILL'S
TO SHAME. I HAVE BOUGHT A NEW PARASOL, PALE BLUE MUSLIN
WITH A AN IVORY FRINGE AND TASSELS, AND TINY BOWS OF
IVORY SATIN AT THE END OF EACH SPOKE. IT IS WILDLY
EXTRAVAGANT BUT HARRIET SAYS EVERYBODY CARRIES THEM IN
BRIGHTON, AND THAT I WILL NEED TO PROTECT MY SKIN, FOR
THE SUN IS FAR HOTTER AT THE SEASIDE, YOU KNOW. BUT I
CANNOT WRITE FOR LONG, FOR I MUST GO AND DRESS. THERE IS
A LITTLE PIECE OF COMMON LAND HERE THEY CALL THE STEINE,
ALL FENCED OFF FOR ELEGANT PROMENADING. I SHALL WEAR
MY NEW GREEN SPRIG, WITH MY PARROT CAPE AND THE SNUFF
GLOVES AND THE BLACK-AND-SILVER NETTED PURSE JANE MADE
ME FOR CHRISTMAS. THEY WILL BE JUST THE THING.

YOUR LOVING DAUGHTER AND SISTER,
LYDIA

SATURDAY, 6TH JUNE

I was tempted to tell the truth, but I could not bear the thought of their smug faces.

I had imagined the sea to be a bright blue, with bobbing sailing yachts and no sound but the cries of bathers, but it is actually gray and angry, with crests of white foam that look like it is spitting. It swells and falls like a living creature, and roars as it crashes on the shore. There are no bathers, the Colonel says, when the sea is in a mood like this. Harriet can't wait to throw herself in when it is calmer, but I do not like it one bit.

The new buildings with their white trim and bow windows are all situated in the new town and monstrous expensive, according to the Colonel. *We* are staying in the old village, which is not nearly as quaint as I wrote in my letter, in Market Street, which is narrow and smells of fish, and each crooked house seems to need the support of the next to stop it tumbling to the ground. My room is the size of our closet at home. Apparently, there are not enough lodgings in Brighton for all the people who want to stay here. "We are lucky not to be sleeping on a floor!" the Colonel says, trying to console Harriet, and I don't think he is joking.

I have a splinter in my foot from a broken floorboard, and my new clothes, which I was so excited about buying for this trip, are a disaster. My dresses are so plain; the necklines that seemed so daring in Meryton are so high! Ladies wear hats here, not bonnets, and daring ruffled pantaloons peeping out from beneath skirts that are a good deal shorter than we wear at home, and I don't know a soul apart from Harriet, because all the men are away on exercises.

If my sisters were here, Jane would help me extract the splinter from my foot. Mary would insist on visiting the library AT ONCE for a fresh supply of books, and Lizzy would walk about like a queen in her unfashionable dresses. Kitty would share my narrow bed and we would joke all through the night about sleeping in a cupboard.

I want home so badly it hurts. And that is the last thing I expected of Brighton.

SUNDAY, 7TH JUNE

*H*arriet burst into my room early this morning. Our landlady, Mrs. Jenkins, told her that the sea was quiet again, and Harriet insisted that we leave immediately to bathe. Sally, her maid, brought coffee and toast as we gathered our belongings into a basket—our swimming shifts, and nets for our hair, and large napkins to dry ourselves afterward, our combs and hairbrushes, additional wraps in case the sun does not shine and our smart new parasols in case it does, a rug for sitting on, and some gingerbread to eat after bathing. We piled it all into the basket so high that Sally could not carry it alone, and we had to unpack half of it again.

Off we struggled, Harriet and I carrying the basket between

us, she in a fashionable ankle-length canary muslin and I in an unfashionably long blue with Sally following behind carrying the rug and napkins, looking like a grumpy little sparrow in her plain dark dress and not in the least bit grateful for her lighter load. Down the dark, fish-smelling street and out into the open of East Cliff, then left along the seafront to the Steine, and I prayed that we would not run into anyone we knew, not just because I was red-faced from the exertion, but because of the dreadful apprehension that had begun to grip me. There was the sea, calmer than when I first saw it, but still swelling and falling like a live creature, still roaring, still the color of lead. There were the bathing machines, preparing to take me into it, and there was my heart, beating at twice its usual speed.

"Hurry *up*, Lydia!" Harriet tugged crossly at the basket handle. "Look how crowded the beach is—we shall never get a bathe if we dawdle."

Down the steps to the beach we climbed, balancing the basket between us, our skirts blowing about our legs, and the roar grew louder.

The air was clammy here, and tasted of salt. I thought that I might be sick.

"Isn't it divine?" Harriet yelled.

It never occurred to me, when I accepted Harriet's invitation, that I would be afraid. All I could think of, looking at the sea, was the Waire—not the stream as it is now, but the raging torrent experienced by my eight-year-old self, clinging to a rock. And they expect me to *swim* in the sea? There are probably millions of drowned people lying on the seabed—sailors and fishermen but also pleasure-seekers just like us who went into the water thinking to amuse themselves and sank straight to the bottom with lungs full of water and eyes like marbles. Even as I write, they are probably being eaten by crabs and little fishes. There is absolutely nothing divine about any of this at all.

The ladies' bathing machines lie to the left of the Steine, the gentlemen's on the right. I knew about these already, of course, from Harriet's descriptions of Weymouth. "They are like dear little caravans," she told me in Meryton. "You skip up a little ladder into them, and then while you change into your bathing dress, the horse pulls you into the sea. Then they unhitch the horse, and you just open the door at the *other* end of the machine and simply dive into the waves!"

In my head, they were gay things the colors of boiled sweets, all pink and green and blue, with cheerful ponies to tow them into the surf. In real life, they are plain and rickety, made of boards like the cart on the farm at home, dragged by long-suffering nags. The large bathing attendants they call dippers, who stand alongside all dressed in navy, look like crows gathered at a watery funeral.

Harriet squinted anxiously down the beach.

"We are too late!" she cried. "The bathing machines are all in the water!"

"I'm sure one will become available presently," I mumbled.

"There is one!" Harriet squealed. "Right at the end, look, Lydia! There is one coming back in!"

Sure enough, right at the end of the line, a machine was lumbering back to the beach through the shallows.

"Sally, run and secure it!" Harriet ordered. She turned to me, a fixed smile upon her face. "Lydia, you must go first. You are my guest. I absolutely insist."

"You go," I whispered. "I promise I don't mind."

"Are you sure?" Harriet was already fumbling in the basket for her shift and napkin.

"Quite sure."

Sally was standing by the returned machine, waving frantically. Harriet grabbed the basket, threw my shift, the gingerbread, and most of my things onto the rug, and ran toward her, clutching her bonnet to her head and her belongings to her bosom.

I sat upon the blanket and drew my knees up to my chin.

If Wickham were here, I surprised myself thinking, he would probably make me walk straight into the sea with my eyes closed, and I wouldn't have time to be afraid.

I chased the thought away. I did not want to think about Wickham.

The shingle crunched. I opened my eyes. Sally had returned, her face redder than ever.

"Missus is gone into the machine." She stood a little to one side, eyeing the gingerbread in its linen cloth.

"Do you want some?" I unwrapped the cake and searched in the basket for the small knife we had packed to cut it. When I looked up, Sally was no longer ogling the gingerbread, but staring behind me down the beach.

"Who is that?" she breathed.

I followed the direction of her gaze. Another machine had come in from the sea a few feet from where we sat, just above the shoreline. A young lady of about Lizzy's age stood in full sun in the doorway, wringing out a tangled mane of fiery copper hair. She wore a dress of the brightest emerald green. A straw basket sat on the floor by her bare feet.

"Did you ever see such a color dress?" Sally whispered. "And silk on a beach, too—covered in sand and salt and whatnot."

The young lady pulled a crumpled yellow bonnet from the basket and jammed it on her head, without pinning up her hair. She should have looked a mess, but she was quite the opposite.

Suddenly, she waved and jumped lightly down onto the beach.

We turned to see where she was going.

A young gentleman was walking toward her, a small black-and-white dog at his side. He was perhaps a couple of years older than me, and a little younger than her. He was about Wickham's height but slighter, with a head of dark curls blowing about in the wind as he waved his hat, and the widest smile upon his face. He was immaculately dressed, in a blue coat and gray breeches and long riding boots, but with a bright red scarf flung dramatically about his throat. The young lady threw herself into his arms and he wrapped the scarf tightly around her shoulders before crushing her to his chest and swinging her round so that her feet clean left the ground. She slipped her hand into his when he set her down again, and together they ran to the water's edge, the little dog leaping at their feet.

They looked as if they owned the entire world.

"Brazen," commented Sally.

"Wonderful," I breathed.

Another machine was creaking back in toward the beach. I sighed, remembering where I was.

"Are you going in, Miss?" asked Sally.

Still the memories of the Waire were too strong.

"Maybe tomorrow," I said. "If the weather continues to improve."

MONDAY, 8TH JUNE

What do I write first? What an evening—oh, what an evening!

I shall start with the theatre.

It is very new and very grand with three stories and two tiers of boxes, and it can seat twelve hundred people. I think that may be more people than I have ever seen together in my life. There were rumors that the Prince himself would attend—Harriet almost fainted when she heard. We didn't even go to the sea today because she had to spend *all day preparing*. The play was a musical thing called *The Weathercock*, and the players were the vastly famous Mr. and Mrs. Kemble, but I hardly took in a word of it because . . . But I mustn't get ahead of myself.

The Colonel had taken a box in the first tier, no less, and he led us straight to it through the crowd. We went up through a narrow paneled staircase, all dark and poky, and then out we emerged into the sumptuous splendor. Then he went back down to talk to some acquaintances, while Harriet and I observed the room.

I never saw such elegance—not even at the Netherfield ball! The Prince did not come, but even if he had, it could not have been a grander affair. Such gleaming bare shoulders and bosoms, such diamonds and pearls and plumage! Ostrich feathers are all the rage here, dyed different colors, and they wave about, tickling people's noses and getting in the way but looking very splendid and fine. Thank goodness Harriet very civilly lent me her old Indian shawl, which is quite as good as her new one, Russian flame trimmed with coquelicot, which looked almost elegant over my white spotted muslin. And thank goodness Mamma insisted that I bring her little gold velvet hat! Straw would not have done here at all. It is hopelessly old-fashioned, of course, but in Munro's (which is quite the smartest shop in Brighton), I found a tremendous coquelicot feather which has absolutely transformed it, and *thank goodness* because . . .

Harriet was using her opera glasses to search the room now, fretting that the Colonel would not return in time for the curtain.

"Oh, look who is here!" she cried.

Four officers had entered the theater. Through the throng,

I caught sight of tall Denny, Carter's ginger hair, Pratt's unfashionable whiskers . . . and Wickham.

I immediately assumed an air of vast indifference, tilting my head *just so* to show off my feather. They approached. They were just beneath the box, going through to the dark staircase. Denny was parting the curtain; they were entering the box . . .

"Mrs. Forster! Miss Lydia!"

In they came, all swagger and smiles.

"At last, some company!" Harriet cried. "We have been quite forlorn without you, have we not, Lydia?"

"Forlorn ladies! We can't have that." Wickham smiled as he leaned over her hand. I crossed *my* hands firmly behind my back.

He bowed to me. I curtsied haughtily and opened my mouth to say something extremely cutting—but no sound came out.

It was utterly mortifying, but then . . . oh, extraordinary, gratifying evening!

Denny glanced out across the floor and exclaimed, "Good Lord!" Wickham looked, too, and the color rose to his cheeks. Carter chuckled and said, "Hell's fire, my friend, you cannot escape the man!"

"It appears not." Wickham forced a smile.

I looked down, toward a party walking beneath us—and fairly gasped with surprise.

For there, towering over the crowd, dressed as usual both more plainly and more finely than all around him—the cut and cloth of his dark gray coat so obviously more expensive, his necktie gleaming more white—was Mr. Darcy! Mr. Bingley, his sisters, and Mr. Hurst all followed in his wake, struggling to keep up with him as he strode toward the stairs. They disappeared, and Wickham breathed—then they re-emerged, <u>in the box next to ours</u>, and Wickham took a discreet step back toward the curtain.

Our box stood between theirs and the stage. In the orchestra pit, the musicians were warming their instruments. Mr. Darcy turned toward them, and his eyes lit immediately on me.

He turned as pale as a ghost—and that is *not* an exaggeration.

"Miss Lydia!" He stared. Then, gathering his wits, bowed.

Mr. Darcy! Bowing at me—*vain, ignorant, idle, and absolutely uncontrolled* Lydia! I curtsied, all smirks, with a sideways glance at Wickham to check that he was watching.

Ask me about Lizzy, I silently urged Mr. Darcy. *I dare you.*

Mr. Darcy coughed. "Your family," he said. "Are they well?"

"Quite well, thank you." I grinned. I waved at Mr. Bingley, who waved cheerily back while his sisters ignored me completely. "I did not know, Mr. Darcy, that you were coming to Brighton. I am sure *my sister* would have sent word to me if she had known. I hear you saw something of her while you were both in Kent."

His eyes flashed dangerously at the mention of Kent. I can only imagine how Lizzy's refusal must have hurt his pride. He is <u>not</u> a man to be crossed.

"I—It is a short visit," he stuttered. (Mr. Darcy stuttered!)

"Miss Bingley's idea. She enjoys the theater, and fashionable company, and there were rumors that the Prince of Wales . . ."

But now Colonel Forster arrived in our box and, recognizing Mr. Darcy and Mr. Bingley from Meryton, came forward with hearty greetings, then introduced his men. Mr. Bingley shook hands amiably with everybody. Darcy's expression darkened at the sight of Wickham, who greeted him with only a slight bow. There was an uncomfortable silence.

"And how do you enjoy Brighton, Darcy?" the Colonel asked.

"Very little," was the short answer, with a glare in Wickham's direction. "I dislike the seaside. I find it is a dangerous place."

I remembered that Mr. Darcy's sister had been at the sea at Ramsgate at the time of her attempted elopement.

But now a hush descended on the theater, and the lights were dimming. The musicians were waiting, bows at the ready, hands poised over keyboards. The conductor raised his baton. The thick red curtain began its ascent, and the evening's performance began.

Though my mind was racing, I kept my eyes riveted on the stage. Only halfway through the first act did I realize that Wickham was seated just behind me, and had leaned forward to whisper in my ear.

"Mr. Darcy seemed very affected when he saw you, Lydia," he murmured.

Suddenly, I wanted him to know everything—to understand that the Bennet girls are capable of attracting suitors far grander and more worthy of them than *he*.

"I daresay he did not expect to see me," I whispered back. "And it was a shock to him, because I reminded him of Lizzy. He is madly in love with her, you know. He has asked her to marry him."

"Indeed!" Wickham sounded startled. Ha! "And has she accepted?"

"She has not," I whispered. That too felt good—telling him that not everyone is like him, ready to marry for money and without love.

"Oh, she will change her mind." For the first time since I have known him, there was not the slightest trace of humor about Wickham's features. "You can be quite certain of that. Darcy always gets what he wants."

"He does not like *you* at all," I said. "Though I suppose that is understandable."

"What can you mean?"

My heart beating faster than ever, I turned and looked him straight in the eyes.

"I know about Georgiana Darcy."

For once, he had nothing to say.

"I shan't tell anyone," I said. "For her sake. But you lied to me, Wickham, when you said you did not pursue Miss King for her money. That is what you do, and I don't like it. I don't like *you*."

He held my gaze, but I did not look away. Slowly, he nodded, and in his eyes I fancy that I read something new—something like respect, which made me swell with pride.

"At last!" I wanted to say. "Do not think you can fool me again!"

Then Harriet glanced toward us with an irritated "Hush!" and I turned my attention once more to the stage, but—as I have already written—I took in very little of the play. The more I thought of it, the more I realized what a very fine thing it would be for Lizzy to marry Mr. Darcy (even though he so rudely criticized me before). How relieved Mamma would be! And if Lizzy married Mr. Darcy, perhaps his friend Mr. Bingley would finally propose to Jane—*that* conundrum is yet to be resolved. And Mary would have infinite access to books, because doubtless Mr. Darcy has an immense library, and Kitty would have infinite access to rich young men from whom to pick a husband, and when we passed Wickham in Lizzy's fine carriage, on our way from a party to a ball, he would see with his own eyes how far we are come and be sorry that he ever treated any of us ill.

I am not sure, looking back, that I should have told him Lizzy's secret. I do not altogether trust him to keep it. But I am not going to think about that now.

TUESDAY, 9TH JUNE

When I woke up this morning all the clouds were gone, the sky was blue, and the sun was shining brightly. Today we did not make so much fuss about the beach. There was no gingerbread and no blanket, no hair nets or additional wraps. We arrived at the beach just in time to watch the bathing machines setting up by the shore, the horses pulling and the horsemen slapping them and the blue-dressed dippers waddling alongside, with children darting in and out between the wagons. It reminded me of when the fair arrives at home, except that instead of music there were the waves and the gulls, and instead of the smell of food there was a warm, salty wind blowing off the water.

The waves were the same blue as the sky, their frilly crests today like trims of lace. Seagulls floated lazily above and there were a few sails out on the water. It was exactly how I had imagined it before I came, and for a moment, looking at it, my heart soared. Then, as we made our way down the steps and toward the machines, it sank again.

"We must be first in the water," Harriet declared. "We will run if we have to. There must be no one before us. You will see, Lydia, how very amusing it is. Why, I never felt better in my life than I did on Sunday after bathing!"

She chose two machines toward the end of the line, farthest from the prying eyes of onlookers. She skipped up the steps into hers without a backward glance, but I stood on the fine shingle looking up at mine with limbs too heavy to move. The machines, the horses, the bathers—how small they looked beside the sparkling sea!

"You going in, Miss?" The dipper was watching me with an impatient frown.

I thought of Wickham, the look of newfound respect in his eyes when I told him I knew about Georgiana Darcy and when I told him about Mr. Darcy's proposal. What would *he* think of my standing here, trembling?

"Yes, I am," I replied, and seized the ladder with both hands.

Inside, the machine was plain but dry, with neat hooks from which to hang my clothes, and a bench on which to sit to change, and curtained windows at the front and back from which to peep at the town or the sea, which made me feel like a little girl again, playing in a den. It would almost have been snug but for the fact that no sooner had I closed the door behind me than it began to move! It is quite one thing to move about when you are in a high-sprung carriage, with nothing to do but sit back and watch the scenery. It is quite another on a pebble beach, being flung this way and that as a horse pulls you into the sea while you attempt to remove all your clothes and don your bathing shift. I tumbled off the bench as I unlaced my boots. Bounced off a wall as I unbuttoned my dress. Staggered about with my bodice round my waist as we came to a sudden stop and began gently to sway.

I struggled out of my dress, hung it on a hook, stepped carefully to the back of the wagon, and parted the muslin curtain. We had come not more than a few yards, but the town looked suddenly very far away—for those few yards were all water. I ran, lurching, to the front window.

Water all around us!

"You ready, Miss?" The dipper (her name is Janet) was growing impatient.

"Almost!" I took my bathing shift from its peg and pulled it over my head. It caught in my hair and again over my shoulder—I had forgotten the buttons.

"Need any help?"

I tugged on the shift. There was a ripping sound. One of the buttons went flying, but at last the wretched thing was on.

"I'm ready!" I shouted, and threw open the door.

The world is very different when you are standing on a mere platform inches above the sea. You cannot see land, and the sea is lapping at your feet, and it would take only one larger-than-average wavelet for the water to rush in and possibly drown you.

I imagine it is a bit like being alone on a very small island.

Or perhaps not *completely* alone.

"You can climb down the steps, Miss, or you can jump." Janet stood up to her thighs in water beside the door.

"If you do jump," she continued, "you're best going lengthways. Like a dive, but without going under. The water's only three foot deep."

"Lengthways?"

"Watch your friend, Miss." Janet nodded to the next machine along, where Harriet had appeared at the top of her steps in her pristine shift.

"Lydia!" She waved. "Isn't it heaven?"

And she flung herself into the water, landing on her belly with a sound like a slapped fish. Janet winced.

"Like that?" I asked.

"Try crouching," she advised. "It'll hurt less."

I stepped down into the water. The waves lapped at my feet, then my ankles and knees. I paused. I craned my neck round the edge of the wagon and looked back at the beach. Most of the machines were in the water now, and everywhere scantily clad ladies were hurling themselves into the waves. I looked back down at my feet. The water was cold. It was *moving*. I couldn't see the bottom. I thought I saw a fish. It might have been a shark. Mary had told me about these fearsome creatures, when she was studying natural history. They can eat you in one gulp.

"I cannot do this," I said.

While I was hesitating, another machine had lumbered to take its position beside mine. The door opened, and I recognized the occupant immediately, by her red hair and also by something else—an indefinable air of owning the entire world.

It was the young lady from the other day—the one with the handsome gentleman friend and the small dog and the extraordinary emerald silk dress. Her bathing attire was no less outlandish. It was not yellow like everyone else's bathing shift, but green like her dress, sleeveless, close-fitting, and cut short above the knee. She stood for a few seconds, still and strong as marble at the top of her steps, with only her shift and hair fluttering in the wind. Then she took a breath, bounced lightly on her feet, and dived headfirst and graceful into the waves. She cut through the water so cleanly the sea never even noticed, but swallowed her without so much as a ripple, and she stayed under so long I was sure she must be drowned. But then up she bobbed again, like the moorhens on the pond at home, and began to swim in strong, steady strokes out into the open water.

"If you've finished gawping," Janet said, "I've other ladies waiting."

And then she pushed me in.

Janet's idea of bathing is to grasp you firmly by the shoulders and push you briskly under the water five times in quick succession, which is just as unpleasant as it sounds. I think I swallowed quite my body weight in seawater this morning, and when I lean forward it *still* pours out of my nose in alarming quantities, but even so IT WAS THE MOST WONDERFUL THING I HAVE EVER DONE IN MY LIFE. Janet didn't give me time to be afraid, and it would have been impossible anyway, with her beside me. She is built like an oak wardrobe, and she did not let go of me once. And oh, the feeling of being in the water, as it swirls you about, and pushes you up, and tumbles you over, and causes your skin to prickle and your eyes to sting and your whole body to come alive. Alive! That is exactly how it made me feel. Alive as I have never been before! Alive as I remember feeling all those years ago when I was a little girl, in those few seconds before I nearly drowned in the Waire.

The red-haired young lady returned from her sea swim as I spluttered up from my final dunking. She grasped the ladder into her bathing machine and, refusing the aid of her dipper, climbed out of the water. I hurried out after her, but it took me even longer to struggle out of my wet shift than it had to change into a dry one. By the time I came back out onto the beach, she had disappeared.

BRIGHTON
TUESDAY, 9TH JUNE

DEAR KITTY,

WE HAVE BEEN SO BUSY SINCE WE ARRIVED, BUT WE FINALLY
GOT AROUND TO BATHING TODAY, AND IT IS EVERY BIT AS
AMUSING AS MARIA'S COUSIN TOLD US. TODAY WAS JUST A
BIT OF GENTLE SPLASHING, BUT I HAVE TOLD MY DIPPER
(A BATHING ATTENDANT) THAT I WANT TO LEARN TO SWIM,
AND SHE SAYS SHE NEVER SAW ANYONE WITH A MORE NATURAL
ABILITY, AND THAT I HAD TAKEN TO THE WATER LIKE AN
ABSOLUTE DUCK! DO NOT TELL MAMMA, BUT I AM ABOUT TO
MAKE CONSIDERABLE CHANGES TO THE BATHING SHIFT SHE
MADE ME. IT IS IMPOSSIBLE TO SWIM PROPERLY WITH ALL
THAT CLOTH FLAPPING ABOUT YOUR LEGS. I AM GOING TO CUT
IT SHOCKINGLY SHORT, AND REMOVE THE ARMS AS WELL!
    WE SAW WICKHAM AT THE THEATER LAST NIGHT. I CAN'T GO
INTO DETAIL, EVEN WITH YOU, FOR IT IS ALL EXTREMELY SECRET,
BUT SUFFICE IT TO SAY THAT I HAVE HIM WRAPPED AROUND MY
LITTLE FINGER, AND ALSO THAT I HAVE A FEELING THAT
ALL WILL BE WELL FOR ALL OF US-WICKHAM SAYS IT IS BOUND
TO END WELL, FOR HE ALWAYS GETS WHAT HE WANTS. LOVE IS
IN THE AIR, KITTY, AND SUCH A LOVE-IT WILL SOLVE
EVERYTHING! I AM ONLY SORRY YOU ARE NOT HERE, TOO. I
THINK THAT IF YOU WERE, I WOULD NOT BE ABLE TO KEEP IT
TO MYSELF. PLEASE SAY YOU FORGIVE ME FOR COMING WITHOUT

YOU? I DO FEEL MONSTROUS ABOUT THAT WHOLE BUSINESS, I
REALLY DO—THOUGH I DO THINK YOU WOULD NOT HAVE ENJOYED
IT WITH YOUR COUGH.

YOUR LOVING SISTER,
LYDIA (WHO IS HALF-MERMAID)

SATURDAY, 13TH JUNE

*T*hey do not come into society—the swimming lady and the dark-haired gentleman. I look for them wherever I go, but have only seen them once more at the beach. She was coming out of her machine as we arrived, and walked straight past us toward the steps cut into the cliff where *he* stood waiting. Harriet thinks she is absurd and very un-English, but I think she is magnificent. She was wearing the emerald dress again. Close up, I saw that it was old, the hemline frayed, and the skirt patched, with a low waist and full skirts more reminiscent of Mamma's wardrobe than my own. She wore a cream-and-purple Kashmir shawl, curiously stylish though ill-assorted to the dress. He wore the same blue coat as the first time I saw him, with his red scarf still wrapped around his throat, as ill-matched to his outfit as the Kashmir shawl was to hers, yet just as dashing. There is something so *poetic* about him—Mary would jeer, but that is exactly the word. The pale face, and the tumbling curls, and the fact that he always carries a book. Perhaps that is why he doesn't swim—poets most probably don't. They are too busy thinking of fine words and rhymes and things like that, unlike Wickham, for example, who swims every day and is burnt dark brown by the sun, with gold glints in his hair, which make him exactly like the sort of pirate who goes about trying to kidnap innocent young girls.

I suppose they must be married, though he is so very young.

We went to dance tonight at the Ship Assembly Rooms, which is a very grand establishment on the seafront, with rooms for cards and assemblies and a new ballroom that is the finest I have ever seen, painted all blue and gold, with double rows of seating at either end and an excellent dance floor, and because it is my birthday and I said I had never tasted it, Denny ordered champagne.

"When the war is finished," he said as he filled my glass, "we will all go to France and bathe in the stuff. But for now, we must content ourselves with merely drinking it, because it is a great deal more expensive here than it is over there."

I defy *anyone* not to look inelegant when they take their first sip of champagne. I was completely unprepared for it. Bubbles exploded on my tongue and up my nose, making me snort, then sneeze, then burst out laughing.

"Good?" Denny grinned.

"Wonderful," I admitted, and he refilled my glass.

Until tonight, I had not spoken to Wickham since the evening at the theater, when I disclosed that I knew the truth about Georgiana, and he has not sought me out. As I sipped my champagne, I was aware of him watching me across the room. I turned away, but soon enough there was a light touch at my elbow, and he was standing beside me. The orchestra was striking up after a pause, a tune I did not know.

"Will you grant me a birthday dance?"

It is not easy to be haughty with Wickham, because he never really appears to notice, but I tried.

"I find I do not care to dance."

"Well, I know that is a lie. Lydia Bennet, not care to dance!"

"I do not care to dance *with you*."

"Ah, that is more serious."

I glared at him. A smile tugged at the corner of his mouth, but he looked grave.

"Come, Lydia," he said. "We are old friends, are we not? I apologize, sincerely and without reserve, for any harm I have done you."

"Not only me."

"You, or any other person."

"And you promise that you will not try to ruin any more young ladies."

"On my honor, I promise."

The dancers were taking their places. The music was irresistible.

"I find I do not care much for your promises," I murmured.

"Lydia!"

"Just one dance," I said, and he led me onto the floor.

I hate to say it, but I had forgotten what fun it is to dance with Wickham. The dance was a waltz, which is quite new, even in Brighton. You have to stand very close to your partner, and he holds your hand, with his other hand around your waist, and you go round and round until your pulse is racing and you feel quite giddy. It is a new dance, and considered quite shocking, but I honestly think all dances should be like that, always.

"Well?" Wickham smiled as it ended. "Am I forgiven?"

He was a little breathless, his hair out of place. Suddenly, I saw him just as I had at Longbourn, that afternoon when he first taught me to ride, pacing about the paddock in his shirtsleeves, patiently exhorting me to sit straight and not to grip so tightly, and I almost relented.

"I will think about it," I said.

The orchestra had abandoned the waltz, and changed back to more familiar reels. I danced with Denny and Carter and Pratt and several others whom I did not know. I danced until my feet hurt and I moved from scarlet coat to scarlet coat until I no longer saw their faces. At one point, I stumbled, thinking I glimpsed a head of dark curls, a red scarf, but when I looked again it was not the poet from the beach but someone altogether different.

What a year it has been since my last birthday, when Mary gave me this diary! How much I have had to write!

I was very much in demand this evening, and I did not speak with Wickham again, but—if he behaves himself and even though he is awful—I think I may forgive him. After all, no one dances as well as he does.

SUNDAY, 14TH JUNE

*L*ast night I had a dream. The whole world was green, and I was underwater with Wickham, trying to waltz, but I couldn't breathe. A hand plunged into the water from above. I thought it must be Janet's and clung to it, but as it dragged me into the light, fire took the place of water, which turned into swirling locks of bright red hair, and a voice told me there was nothing to be afraid of. I smiled in my dream, thinking the voice belonged to the young lady from the beach, but then it became Darcy, saying "The seaside is dangerous, Lydia," and I was back in the sea of green, which now was the flooded woods of Longbourn, and the red-haired young lady was swimming away with her mermaid strokes, and the forest stretched for miles as my voice echoed from tree to tree, calling for her to come back. I woke with a single thought—that I must go to the sea and learn to swim.

Harriet says she never sleeps well after champagne. "It is the acidity," she says, though I think it is more to do with how many gallons she drank. Either way, she has forgotten her vow to swim every day and would not stir from her bed this morning.

"Then I shall go alone," I declared.

Well, that did *not* go down well. What would she say to my poor mother, Harriet cried, if a French frigate came suddenly into the bay and sailed away with me to Calais? The French were notorious kidnappers! Or what if Janet should take it upon herself to drown me? With no one to attend me, I could be dead or gone for hours before she found out.

"And besides," Harriet added. "How shall I amuse myself when you are not here?"

"Do you mean when I am dead and drowned, or just while I am bathing?"

"Oh, Lydia!"

She is beginning to sound exactly like my sisters.

I never was more fidgety in my life than lazing about the house this morning. The need to be outside, to shake off the dream, was like an itch. I could not lie on Harriet's bed to read to her as she requested, or lounge on the sofa in the parlor, but paced about the tiny house and twitched the curtains and was all in all so successfully irritating that after an hour Harriet begged me, please, "to go out and not come back until you can be still."

"You are quite impossible," she groaned.

"You are not the first to say that," I admitted as I fled.

Down the street I hurried, clutching my bundle of bathing things (I have quite done away with the cumbersome basket). Along East Cliff, where a brisk wind whipped my skirts about my legs, toward the beach. The sea was another color again today. Darker blue, with sharp frilled crests and spray blowing everywhere and a thick blue band on the horizon. For a moment, I forgot all about the young lady and gentleman and green dresses and dreams. That is the way, I am finding, when you look at the sea. There is only . . . it. Even though I have had several swimming lessons now with Janet, I still can't quite shake away the fear. I tightened my grip on my bundle and headed toward the steps, but I never made it to the beach.

I had to step aside at the top of the steps to make way for a lady coming up. As I waited, I chanced to look over my shoulder, and I saw—*them*. I recognized him first. In his fitted blue coat and with the red scarf still about his throat, he is unmistakable. She no longer looked like a mermaid, but wore an elegant striped dress of dark *corbeau* green and white, with a trim jacket of red velvet, her hair coiled and twisted beneath a large white hat fastened beneath her chin with a matching red ribbon. Together they came out of the apothecary's shop, and walked across the street to where a local boy stood holding a plain black trap hitched to a single gray mare. The gentleman held out his hand as the young lady sprang lightly onto the high seat, then climbed in after her and took the reins. The mare set off at a trot toward the Steine.

"Don't go," I whispered. And then, like the answer to a prayer, a very smart dark-gray curricle drew up beside me and a familiar voice called down.

"Miss Lydia Bennet! What are you doing out by yourself on this fine morning?"

I looked up. Wickham, very politely, tipped his hat.

"Help me up!" I cried. "And follow that trap!"

For all his faults, I must admit that Wickham is excellent in emergencies. His reaction to girls leaping into his curricle and ordering him to give chase to perfect strangers is not, as a normal person's would be, to ask "Why?" or "Are you quite mad?" Not in the least. Wickham's reaction to my dramatic appearance by his side was to crack his whip with a merry "Aye-aye, Captain!" and immediately obey.

It was not easy. In the time that passed between the trap driving away and Wickham and I giving chase, every other vehicle in Brighton appeared to have come out into the street—farmers' carts and fishmongers' trolleys, fashionable landaus and heavy-looking coaches, gentlemen on horseback and ladies in open carriages—the whole lot of them. I had to stand up from my seat to keep the black trap in sight.

"Wickham!" I cried, pointing down Marine Parade. "They are getting away!"

"Hold on to your bonnet," he said, and then, I don't know

how he did it, but Wickham is obviously a horse-handling genius, for by nudging and shuffling and barging his way forward, with a flick of his whip here and a slap of the reins there, with a smile and a tip of his hat and a series of cheery apologies, he had us clear of that jam and onto the open road in no time at all.

"Faster now, my beauties!" Wickham cracked his whip, and we tore along at a smart trot. I squealed. People stared. As the traffic thinned, he urged the horses on again and faces and buildings became a blur.

"Excellent sport!" Wickham called over the wind. "I must rescue you more often!"

"Can you see them?" I shouted.

"Straight up ahead! We are gaining on them. What's the plan, Lydia?"

"I don't know!" I cried. "Just keep chasing!"

"Whoa, there!" Wickham pulled on the reins. The horses slowed to a trot. "What do you mean, you don't know? Lydia, what are we actually doing here?"

I realized that I hadn't a clue.

The horses settled into a walk. Wickham assumed a pious expression that did not suit him.

"I really don't think I can allow this behavior, Lydia. As an old friend, I have a duty to your family . . ."

"Be quiet!"

Up ahead, the trap was turning.

"I am merely trying to protect you . . ."

"No, be *quiet*. Look! They are leaving the road! Oh, Wickham! Hurry!"

"Only because I am curious," he said, and whipped the horses into a trot again.

The turning was a narrow climbing track. Wickham peered at it dubiously.

"Take it," I ordered.

"This is not my curricle, you know," he said. "It's Denny's new toy. I beat him last night at whist, and this was his stake."

"His *curricle*?"

"Just for a few days. If I damage it I shall have to pay, and those hedgerows look monstrous close."

"Wickham, please . . ."

He sighed, and clicked his tongue at the horses.

The track was dark from overhanging trees, and very steep. I found myself leaning forward as the horses climbed, willing them on until at last the incline softened and the trees thinned, and we found ourselves on a wide and level track at the top of the hill, with the downs spread out on either side of us, beyond hedgerows bursting with poppies and daisies and cow-parsley.

"You see!" I said. "It's pretty."

"Very." Wickham smiled. Though the trap before us had only one horse, its driver had the advantage of knowing the road. There was no sign of it when we crested the hill. I stood up in the curricle, leaning on Wickham for balance and, shielding my eyes from the sun, surveyed the horizon, but I could not see them anywhere.

"Whoa!" Wickham brought the horses to a sudden halt, and I fell back hard onto the seat.

"What did you do that for?"

He pointed. "Look."

We had stopped by a simple wooden gate, with peeling paintwork, flanked by two pillars on each of which sat, somewhat incongruously, a small stone elephant. One was almost entirely obscured by foxgloves. The other elephant bore a wooden sign about its neck that read *Tara*—presumably the name of the property that lay beyond. Underneath, in black paint, someone had added the words "Enter, traveler, if ye dare."

I made Wickham hold the horses steady while I stood again in the hope of seeing more. A track led away from the gate through an overgrown meadow, and disappeared over the brow of the hill.

"Will you tell me now who it is we are chasing?" he asked.

"I don't honestly know," I admitted. "Do you think we can go in?"

"We can," he said. "Though with no invitation and no idea who we are going to see it might not make a good impression."

I sat back down and sighed. Beside me, Wickham was chuckling.

"What are you laughing at?" I snapped.

"You, Lydia. You never cease to surprise me. You are a young lady of mystery."

"Oh, stop being ridiculous and drive."

He took up the reins. "Home?" he asked. "Or while we are out, shall we explore?"

I hesitated, thinking of Harriet, and the dark parlor with the smoking fire.

"If you are very good," Wickham said, "I may even let you drive."

We did explore, and Wickham did let me drive. The wind up on the downs unsettled the horses, and they sprang into a gallop at the merest tickle of the whip. I cannot imagine how loud my screams must have been—very, I think, from the look on Wickham's face. By the time he took the reins from me to slow us down, my bonnet was hanging by its ribbons, my hair was all undone, and I was quite out of breath.

Wickham hitched the horses to a tree and together we walked to the edge of the cliff. It was not very high—a dozen feet at most. I thought that the drop to the sea would be sheer, but when we looked over the edge I saw that some of the land had dropped already, and fell away in tiers toward the water. It was beautiful: white chalky soil, bright green grass, gorse in full golden flower, the clear blue of the sky and a wide cove of sapphire water so clear I could see right to the bottom.

"It is like a completely different sea," I breathed.

"It might not be England at all," Wickham said. "It is just like the Mediterranean."

"Is it really?"

"Yes and no. Fancy a swim?"

His gaze met mine, wicked and amused. When Wickham

looks at you that way, as if he is laying down a challenge, it is almost irresistible. For a second, I thought I might do it—scramble down the cliff to throw myself into that beautiful sparkling sea. But then—and probably just as well—there came the sound of bells and baaing and a hundred cloven feet, and a flock of sheep came round the bend in the road, followed by a dog and a shepherd. Wickham ran to move the horses. The shepherd touched two fingers to his cap. Wickham responded with a good-natured salute, and we climbed back into Denny's curricle.

"Enter, traveler, if ye dare," I said as we passed the gates to Tara. "Don't you think that's intriguing?"

"Most," he agreed.

It was only as he drove away, with a flourish of his whip, after he set me down again near the Battery, that I remembered what he called me when we first saw the gates.

A young lady of mystery.

I like that.

Longbourn
Thursday, 11th June

Dear Lydia,
Happy birthday for Saturday! We are so busy here trying
to console Mamma and Kitty for your absence, and I have
so much to do to prepare for my own trip north (Aunt and
Uncle have invited me to join them in a tour of the Lakes and
we set out in a fortnight), that I fear this may not reach
you in time. I hope you had a very happy day! Sixteen
years old! I hope that you are behaving yourself, now that
you are all grown-up. I am enclosing a pretty scrap of
lace—I hope you like it better than last year's ribbon!
    Seriously, Liddy. Kitty says you are having
a splendid time, and are learning to swim, and that
Brighton is all you hoped it would be (she cried quite a
lot as she told me—perhaps another letter soon, with some
seaside trinket to cheer her up?). But I hope you are being
sensible. You know you are so easily led, and with no
big sister to watch over you, I do worry. Please promise
your head will not be turned by the first person you
happen to admire.
    Write again soon, with details of bathing! We are
vastly envious.

                        Your affectionate sister,
                        Lizzy

TUESDAY, 16TH JUNE

I thought of burning Lizzy's letter. Then I pasted it into my diary to remind me how annoying she is.

Tonight was cards in the Ship Assembly Rooms, and Harriet insisted on dressing me. She pretended it was a friendly gesture, but I know very well that it was actually a secret act of revenge, because she is annoyed with me for "making a spectacle of myself," as she has it.

"Galloping about with Wickham!" she cried this morning over breakfast. "Terrorizing all of Brighton with a pair of runaway horses!"

There are no secrets in this town.

"We did not *gallop*," I lied. "Wickham was in complete control absolutely all the time. Nobody was terrorized."

"What will people say about *me* if you behave like this? I shall have to write to your parents, and then they will call you away, and what will *I* do with no companion?"

It is typical of Harriet to be more concerned for her reputation than for mine, and I think she is far too lazy to write to my parents, but I must be more careful.

"You are right," I said meekly. "I didn't think, you know, because Wickham is an old family friend, but it was quite wrong of me, and most unladylike. I promise I shan't do it again."

The dress she chose for me was pink.

Now, a strong pink the color of sunset, that is almost orange or red, is a very fine thing. A person of my complexion, fair-skinned and blue-eyed, needs to be careful with it, but used in the appropriate manner—a ribbon, a shawl—it can add a certain warmth. Worn with caution, a good pink can be pretty and delightful, but it should never—ever—constitute the main element of any outfit. Not for anyone over the age of ten. Sophy and Philadelphia Gardiner are both wild for the color pink, and there, I believe, I rest my case.

The pink Harriet chose for me tonight was just the tint my cousins favor, pale and pretty and the precise shade to drain all color from my face. Hill makes a summer pudding that is the exact same color.

It is delicious, but no one in their right mind would choose to *wear* it.

Harriet's pink muslin is the clothing embodiment of Hill's dessert, all layers of frills and lace, with a foamy raspberry bodice and skirts the color of strawberries crushed into cream. Just looking at it made the skin of my neck come out in matching blotches, but I wore it without complaining, just to keep her happy.

"Don't you look delightful," Wickham said when he joined us with Carter, Denny, and Pratt at the assembly rooms. "Like a strawberry trifle."

I scowled. The officers laughed. Wickham offered me his arm and whispered, "Come, Lydia! Strawberry trifle just happens to be my favorite. Stop looking so cross, and let us try our luck at a friendly game of lottery tickets, as we did the first time we met in Meryton."

"Very well," I relented. "I will play with you. But only because I beat you the last time we played."

"If I recall, I allowed you to win."

I hit his arm, and he chuckled, and we were turning together toward the tables when . . .

"Monsieur le Comte de Fombelle-Aix-Jouvet!" the master of ceremonies announced. "Mademoiselle la Comtesse de Fombelle-Aix-Jouvet, Mrs. John Lovett, and Miss Esther Lovett!"

Pratt, who was already at the champagne, started to wave his bottle around, hiccoughing, "Moosiour and Mad'mazel the Comte de tra-la-la" over and over and giggling.

"Oh for heaven's sake," Harriet said. "Have some respect for persons of rank. These are titled nobles."

"Rank?" Denny objected. "What do the French nobility have left, that the Revolution has not taken from them?"

I didn't hear Harriet's response. I wasn't listening. I had removed my hand from Wickham's arm and stood alone, staring at the new arrivals.

It was the couple from the beach.

The young man—a count!—wore a gray coat over an embroidered gold waistcoat, his black curls already escaping the blue ribbon meant to hold them back. I have the feeling that he does not overly care for fashion. There is something in the unruly curls, the knot of his cravat, and the hang of his coat that suggests a certain impatience and lack of interest in his appearance, yet for all his rumpled looks he was more glamorous tonight than any other man in the room. And *she* was dazzling in shimmering silver gauze with long white gloves above her elbows and a dark velvet ribbon about her neck, her red hair piled on her head, and an amused expression on her face. Together, they were the embodiment of elegance and sophistication. Their companions, a girl in washed-out lilac and a stout woman who dressed like Mamma, were almost invisible beside them.

I looked around for Wickham. Like me, he stood a little apart from the others, gazing at the new arrivals.

"It's them," I whispered. "The people from the house."

"Plus companions." Perhaps they felt our stare then, too, because the two young women turned their gaze on us. The young lady from the beach—the Comtesse—did not look at Wickham but stared straight at me, and I am quite certain I saw her eyes widen at the sight of my dress. And no wonder. *I* would be amazed if I were her, and saw me. I would probably not be able to believe that people such as I even existed.

Behind me, Denny and Carter were sniggering.

"Lieutenant Wickham strikes again," Denny was saying, and Wickham was telling them to go away (only not so politely).

I dragged my eyes away from the Comte and Comtesse. The mousy girl—Miss Esther Lovett—was still staring at our group, a warm blush spreading across her cheeks. I glanced at Wickham, then back at the girl. She had averted her gaze, but I recognized the look on her face—dazed and confused, a little stupid. When you grow used to him, as I have, you forget the effect that Wickham has on ladies when they first lay eyes on him. I have seen that look many times before—on the face of Mary King, on Lizzy, and even—though I hate to remember it—on myself.

Thank goodness I am quite recovered from *that* phase!

"Who is she?" Harriet asked.

Denny explained that Miss Lovett was currently the most eligible young lady in Brighton, having a fortune of fifteen thousand pounds from her late father, as well as a small estate in Shropshire, there being no male heir.

"How do you know?" I asked. Denny shrugged, and said that this was Brighton. Everyone knew everything about everybody.

"I suppose she stays in the new buildings," Harriet said with a sniff.

Denny said that he had heard they were staying with their French relatives slightly out of town. The house on the hill, I thought. Tara. Did Wickham know already, when we went there yesterday? He stood staring thoughtfully at the party as they retreated to the card rooms.

"You promised," I whispered to him. "On my birthday— you said you wouldn't pursue any more heiresses . . ."

I hid in a smaller room, playing vingt-et-un with Harriet and some other ladies, torn between wanting to see the Comte and Comtesse and not wanting to be seen in my dreadful pink dress.

I will never let Harriet pin so much as a ribbon to my hat again.

Monsieur le Comte and Mademoiselle la Comtesse de Fombelle . . . I made Carter look in the visitor book so that I should know how to write their names. *Monsieur le Comte and Mademoiselle la Comtesse.*

Mademoiselle—I have hardly any French, but I have enough to understand *that*.

Mademoiselle means she is not married. They must be brother and sister!

WEDNESDAY, 17ᵀᴴ JUNE

*T*he sky was milky as I made my way down the steps to the beach this morning, but the air was still and the day already warm. There were not many people yet in the water. I picked my way as fast as I could to Janet's wagon at the far end of the line. This morning I wasted no time but changed into my shift in minutes, then threw myself in the water before Janet had time to catch me.

"I have questions," I said as I came up for air.

"I thought you wanted to learn to swim," she said as she grabbed me by the shoulders.

"Please, wait!" But I only had time to pinch my nose between my fingers before she pushed me underwater again. I flailed about swallowing pints of sea before I remembered what she had taught me, kicked the bottom, and rose to the surface, where I filled my lungs with air, and lay flat on my back, gently paddling my hands and feet.

"Better," Janet grunted. "Now, onto your front and let's practice moving forward."

I felt very proud this morning, because I managed to advance several feet before going under again. Janet is a hard teacher, but she seemed pleased. I think she may even like me, because after my lesson, when I pulled myself up to the machine, she came and sat beside me on the step, and together we looked out over the immense blue of the sea.

"What do you know of the Comtesse de Fombelle?" I asked.

"The lady with the shift that you have copied?"

I reddened, and said, "The very same."

"She's a good swimmer."

"Other than that."

"French," Janet said. "Though she's not been back there since she ran away as a little girl."

"Ran away?"

"From the Revolution." Janet nodded. "Escaped dressed as a peasant with her mamma and brother after the rebel murderers killed her father. They say her mamma rowed them over to England herself in a boat she stole right under a fisherman's nose, and burned it when she got here so they couldn't take her back."

"What did they do to her father?"

Janet drew a finger across her throat with a ghoulish grin.

"Shot or guillotined or starved in prison, who knows? But she didn't hang around long, the mother. Cast off her widow's weeds before it were decent, then married Mr. John Shelton."

"Who is John Shelton?" My head was spinning with all this information.

"Tailor's son, common as any of us till he went off to India to make his fortune. No one knew him when he came back, he were that fine. Too good for the rest of us, built that daft house up on the cliff, lording it about. Then, two years after marrying, he went back out to India, taking his wife and stepchildren with him."

"The Comte and Comtesse de Fombelle . . ." I said.

Harriet had finished her bathe and was on the beach, calling to me to hurry.

"You'd better get back in the water if you don't want to go," Janet said.

I slipped off the steps like an obedient child and splashed about for a bit.

"So who are Mrs. and Miss Lovett?"

"Mrs. Lovett is their aunt by marriage," Janet said. "Mr. John's sister, who married a lawyer and went off to London, and never a word to say anymore to them she grew up with. Miss Esther Lovett is their stepcousin."

"And where are Mr. and Mrs. Shelton now?"

"He's in India, she's dead."

"Dead?"

"From one of them fevers they have over there. They say he's

160

gone mad with grief, and won't ever come home, but the young gentleman's to start at Oxford soon, and the lady won't leave her brother."

Harriet shouted again. Janet floated off the step with surprising daintiness, and shoved my head underwater one last time.

"That's you done," she said. "Now hurry up and dress, I've other customers waiting."

‿୧୨‿

"At last!" Harriet huffed as I hurried out of the machine. "Mrs. Conway was here, and has invited us to join her for chocolate. Run, Lydia, or we shall miss her!"

Mrs. Conway is one of Harriet's new friends from last night's card party, vastly smart. Harriet is monstrous impressed with her, and fairly sprinted down the beach in her rush to join her at the coffee shop. I said my bootlaces needed tying and that I would catch up with her. I took my time about the laces, hoping for a glimpse of the Comtesse de Fombelle, but she was not on the beach.

India! I thought, as I walked slowly toward the steps. France! Revolution and running away and disguises and executions! My head was still full of their story as I climbed back up to the street.

How could I meet these extraordinary people? What would I say to them if I did?

I almost tripped over a child as I reached the top of the steps. He was running at full pelt along the cliff, ignoring the nursemaid who followed, shouting at him to stop. I jumped aside to avoid him. On he thundered, his little legs pumping at full speed, his head down, faster than seemed possible for one so small. The nursemaid was already tiring. "Master Edward!" She held her sides, blowing and gasping for breath. "Master Edward, come back here at once!"

All along the cliff, heads were turning. A few gentlemen tried to catch the runaway, but he dodged them with ease, until *oomph!* Straight into a tall, booted figure he ran, and stopped dead. For a moment, he was perfectly still. Then he raised his little head, and I followed the direction of his gaze—up at the face that looked gravely down at him.

It was Mr. Darcy, returned from a bathe and looking more disheveled than I have ever seen him, his shirtfront damp, his hair still wet, his face hale and burned from the sun and wind. He actually looked rather handsome, and much more jolly than usual. Perhaps if Lizzy saw him like that she would accept him after all.

The child recovered his wits and attempted to run. Mr. Darcy lifted him neatly from the street and held him in his arms, waiting for the nursemaid to catch up. He turned with him toward the sea, pointed to the colored sail of one of the pleasure boats, then toward a flock of gulls circling a fishing vessel. The child giggled. Mr. Darcy smiled, and his face was transformed—no longer stern and cold, but friendly and soft and almost playful.

The nursemaid ran up, thanked Mr. Darcy, and walked away, scolding the child and holding him tightly by the hand. Mr. Darcy watched them go, then, turning in my direction, started. He bowed.

"Miss Lydia."

I curtsied. "Mr. Darcy."

"You have been bathing?"

"I have! I am learning to swim." I could not resist a boast. "I am become shockingly good at it, too."

"But you are alone?"

"Mrs. Forster is waiting for me in the coffee shop."

"Indeed . . . indeed . . ." He hesitated, searching for the right words. "My best regards to your sisters," he said at last. "I mean, to your family. Your mother and father . . ."

"I know what you mean." I smiled.

I never thought that anything Mr. Darcy did would make me laugh, but he actually blushed when I said that. We talked for a few minutes of this and that, then he took his leave and hurried away.

Mr. Darcy is leaving for London tomorrow, he told me, and from there to Derbyshire later in the summer. I rather wish now that he would return to Meryton, and try proposing to Lizzy again. I think he might make a fine husband for her, even though *he* is not a count.

BRIGHTON
WEDNESDAY, 17TH JUNE

DEAR KITTY,

BRIGHTON IS BETTER AND BETTER-YOU WOULD NOT BELIEVE THE
SORT OF PEOPLE WHO ARE HERE! THE VERY ESSENCE OF
SMARTNESS AND NOBILITY. I AM PLOTTING AND PLANNING HOW
TO MEET THEM EVEN AS I WRITE!
    A FEW DAYS AGO, I WENT ON A DRIVE WITH WICKHAM
AMONG THE CLIFFS. WE STUMBLED UPON A LITTLE BEACH WITH
WATER THE COLOR OF LADY LUCAS'S SAPPHIRE BROOCH, AND
WICKHAM SAID IT WAS JUST LIKE THE MEDITERRANEAN-IMAGINE
SAILING ABOUT ON A WHOLE SEA THE COLOR OF JEWELS! THAT
IS WHAT I WOULD DO IF I WERE RICH AND NOBLE.
    BY THE WAY, THE SECRET I WAS TELLING YOU ABOUT-BY
WHICH I MEAN THE ONE I CAN'T TELL YOU-IS BECOME QUITE
EXCITING, AND THE GENTLEMAN APPEARS AS ENAMORED AS
EVER. I AM SORRY TO BE SUCH A LADY OF MYSTERY, BUT WHEN
THE SECRET IS REVEALED, YOU WILL UNDERSTAND WHY!

                YOUR ENIGMATIC SISTER,
                LYDIA

PS: I ENCLOSE A RIBBON YOU MIGHT LIKE.

PPS: PLEASE COULD YOU ASK MARY IF INDIA IS ON THE
MEDITERRANEAN SEA?

SATURDAY, 20TH JUNE

he truth is I had no idea how to go about meeting the de Fombelles. I thought and thought about it, and in the end appealed to Wickham for advice.

"Me? Why do you think I can help you?"

"You are so good at arranging to meet with people you shouldn't."

Wickham looked blank.

"Georgiana Darcy!" I hissed. "Mary King!"

"Very well." He sighed. "I will see what I can do."

That was two days ago. Yesterday, when we met on the Steine, he told me that, having succeeded in bribing Mrs. Lovett's maid, he had the information I needed.

"The Comte and Comtesse de Fombelle plan to visit the Chalybeate Spa in Hove tomorrow afternoon," he told me. "They will arrive at two o'clock with their cousin Miss Esther Lovett, who is recovering from a cold and whose mother wishes her to take the chalybeate waters."

"That is it? That is your information? But what should I do?"

"Go to the spa and plan your strategy when you get there. I'm sure you'll think of something."

Harriet insisted on accompanying me to the spa with Mrs. Conway. "Taking the waters is vastly fashionable, my dear," she explained as we hurried to meet her new friend's carriage outside the library. "Only a few pennies per glass, and Mrs. Conway says you never felt better afterward. Oh, this is an excellent plan of yours, Lydia."

She was still chattering excitedly as we entered the spa gardens, and Mrs. Conway was just as loud. I prayed that I should not be with them if we met the Comte and his party, then felt a little ashamed, because it is exactly the sort of thing someone like Caroline Bingley would think.

"At least today I am properly dressed," I told myself. It rained yesterday, and I spent the afternoon taking up my blue muslin, adding a broad lace frill to the neck and a row of tucks to the hem, with matching lace on my bonnet, and I have splashed out on a pair of frilly pantaloons to wear peeping out beneath. I think I have been vastly clever. The whole *toilette* looks delightful, especially with my little tan spencer and new parasol. I felt extremely confident as we set out from Brighton, but as we arrived, my assurance faltered.

The path was not wide enough for three. I trailed along behind Harriet and Mrs. Conway, my eyes darting left and right in the hope of spotting the Comte and Comtesse, and I confess I was quite despairing of ever seeing them when suddenly—a flash of scarlet, a shadow of blue caught my eye within a shady bower, a few feet from the path.

The Comte! Seated upon a bench, reading a book, his red scarf about his neck.

"Harriet!"

She stopped with an impatient sigh.

"What is it, dear?"

"I feel so tired, all of a sudden. Would you mind awfully if I sat upon this stone bench and waited for you here?"

"I will take you home" (through clenched teeth, with an anxious glance at Mrs. Conway).

"Oh, pray do not trouble yourself! I shall be *quite* happy here. Please, do go on to the fountain. I shall be delightfully comfortable sitting here in the shade."

Mrs. Conway insisted that she must bring back some water for me. I begged her to take her time, and drooped upon the bench, the picture of ladylike exhaustion, until they were out of sight. My first instinct, I admit, was to rush forward the second they disappeared and simply see what happened. But, *Plan your strategy*, Wickham had said. I had not much time—it must be used to its maximum advantage. I needed to plan my campaign. I needed to *think*.

The first thing to do, I told myself (strategizing like a soldier), was to make quite sure he was alone. Rushing in to overpower him, only to be confronted, without a plan, by Miss Lovett and the Comtesse, would mean being outnumbered and put me at a disadvantage. I looked left, then right. The alley in which I found myself was deserted. Walking as fast as I could while still maintaining an air of nonchalance, I left the path and came to stand behind his bower, feigning interest in a pretty climbing rose twisting round a conveniently placed arch. I peeped through the foliage. The Comte was engrossed in his book. His sister and Miss Lovett were nowhere to be seen.

Think, Lydia, think! What did I know about him?

He reads (not to be helped). He dresses well (if carelessly— he had thrown his gloves down on the bench beside him), with a touch of drama (the scarlet scarf), and I noticed a rip in his jacket, beautifully mended but visible nonetheless. He is French, he is a nobleman, he lived in India . . .

Gloves!

My heart beating wildly, I slipped through the rose-bedecked arch, discreetly tugging off one of my own gloves (white kid, gray buttons—adorable). Advancing toward him, I occupied myself with searching through the contents of my reticule. Then, as I drew level with him, I let the glove fall at his feet.

"Lord, what a clumsy fool I am!"

He was not reading at all. He was asleep—asleep! I had not

bargained on that. As he started awake with a cry of alarm, his book fell from his hands. It came to rest beside my glove and there—*there*—I spotted my chance.

Oh, blessed Mr. Collins and his boring readings at Longbourn! For the book was none other than his old favorite— *The Meditations of Saint Augustine.*

Crouching to retrieve my glove, I picked up the book and held it out to the Comte. "Dear Saint Augustine," I murmured. "I'm afraid he also took a bit of a tumble."

"Is he dear?" The Comte rubbed the sleep from his eyes as he stood up, looking somewhat confused. "I'm afraid I find him rather heavy-going."

"The world is a book," I quoted airily. *"And those who do not travel read only one page. I* could read him for hours!"

"Could you really?" He looked at me doubtfully. I batted my eyelids with a demure smile, and he began to laugh. He looks so nice when he laughs! It makes his eyes sparkle. "You are joking. Thank God! I honestly think this is the dullest thing that I have ever read, but I am going up to Oxford next term and my tutor gave me a pile of ghastly books to read before I left India, which he swears are absolutely indispensable to my survival. I prefer poetry myself, and plays and novels. How clever you are to know about him, though. My sister has no idea."

"Has no idea about what?" drawled a female voice behind us, and then there *she* was, with Miss Lovett by her side.

The Comtesse was splendid in her striped *corbeau* green and white again, this time with a stiff saffron jacket and ribbon on her wide-brimmed hat. The tiny black-and-white dog barked ferociously at the end of a short leash, a matching saffron ribbon about its neck. Her cousin, who is tiny with huge dark eyes, looked like a timid vole by her side. She wore plain cambric with a dull brown spencer, and was carrying a cup of water.

"My sister, Théodorine de Fombelle, and my cousin Miss Esther Lovett," said the Comte. "But please, what is your name?"

I told them.

"Miss Lydia Bennet!" the Comte cried, like it was the most pleasing name he had ever heard. "Miss Lydia Bennet, who reads Saint Augustine."

"Goodness," his sister said. She sat down upon the bench with her little dog, and kissed its nose to stop it barking. "That is impressive. I bet Esther's read Saint Augustine, too, haven't you, Esther?" Miss Lovett blushed, and said she had.

"And I bet you haven't," the Comte teased.

The Comtesse ignored her brother's jibe, but turned away from the dog to scrutinize me. "So you're clever," she said. "And wearing rather a good dress, today. An infinite improvement on that pink creation the other night."

"Theo!" her brother exclaimed.

"But that wasn't yours. I'm right, am I not? I said that it was borrowed. It was much too tight about the bodice, and loose about the skirts. Also, too fussy. This"—she indicated my new dress—"this is much more your style. Fitted, and amusing—the pantaloons a slightly obvious touch perhaps, but *piquant* never-theless. Not, you will forgive me, *cloying*. No, I rather think that pink thing belonged to the lady you accompanied. The color would have suited her darker complexion, and from her *toilette* that night it is obvious she has a taste for furbelows. The parasol is Munro's, of course. He has been selling them by the dozen since the good weather arrived."

The Comtesse's voice never stays the same. It swoops from fast and natural to slow and almost affected in an instant and without apparent reason. Her accent, like her brother's, is an inconsistent mixture, veering in her short speech from English to French to a singsong lilt I assume must be a legacy from India.

"Well?" she demanded. "Is it Munro's?"

"It is," I admitted, feeling a little light-headed.

"My cousin is a talented dressmaker," Esther Lovett murmured. "There is nothing she does not know about fashion."

"You should see her workroom," the Comte said. "It is quite professional."

"I don't like to do anything by half," the Comtesse informed me. "As for the parasol, my advice is to throw it out. Parasols are only good for playing cricket on the beach, and that one is particularly offensive."

"Theo!" the Comte exploded. Even Miss Lovett looked shocked, but I could think of only one thing.

How could I see them again?

"I should love to see your workroom," I blurted.

"Then you must come!" the Comte cried. "Mustn't she, Theo?"

For a short second, I thought I saw her hesitate. But then,

"Of course, come!" She pulled a calling card from the minuscule black reticule that hung from her wrist. "Come next week, on Thursday. We're out on the cliffs."

"At what time . . ."

"Come for tiffin," the Comte said.

"He means luncheon," Esther whispered. "Around midday."

"Al will fetch you."

"Al?"

"Alaric." The Comtesse nodded at her brother. "Now, Esther—are you going to drink this disgusting water or not? You cannot carry that cup about with you forever. Just glug it down, there's a good girl."

Miss Lovett pulled a face as she peered at the brownish water in her cup, but I can see already that it is not possible to refuse her cousin. A few drops dribbled down her chin as she drank, and she blushed as the Comte very gallantly offered her his handkerchief, after which the ladies curtsied and took their leave. The Comte tipped his hat, followed them, then ran back.

"Please forgive my sister," he said. "She is always frighteningly direct."

"No! It is not . . . I mean . . . I have seen her swim at the beach. I think she is perfectly splendid."

It was the sort of unguarded, unthinking remark that would make Mary or Lizzy roll their eyes in disbelief, but the Comte de Fombelle beamed as if he couldn't agree more.

"And I think it's perfectly splendid that you know Saint Augustine," he said, in a voice ringing with sincerity.

"Oh, yes!" I said. "I mean, I adore him."

"I must run after them—but we will see you very soon. I will be at the Coach and Anchor at eleven o'clock. You will come, won't you?"

"Of course!"

My head spun as I watched him hurry away, and I had to sit down on the bench.

I have met them at last. Good grief! The Comte even appears to like me. But oh Lord—what tangled web of lies have I begun to weave?

Longbourn,
Friday, 19th June

Dear Lydia,

I hope you are well and still enjoying the delights of sea-bathing.

Wickham is entirely wrong to compare the South Coast to the Mediterranean. The Mediterranean is a sea full of flying fish and dolphins and porpoises, lined with countries of vast and ancient historical interest. In Greece there are also temples, and it is one of the few places that I should like to see very much. And the answer to your question is no, India is nowhere near to the Mediterranean. I continue to be appalled by your lack of education.

Your sister,
Mary

PS: do not be surprised if Kitty does not answer you. The ribbon you sent in your last letter was much appreciated, but she is still angry.

SUNDAY, 21ST JUNE

My lack of education, as Mary calls it, is entirely Father's fault. There's no point blaming Mamma. She knows even less about anything than I do. But Father, who spends whole days in his library, could have taught me *something*. If we had been boys, we should all have been sent to school, but I don't see what being a boy has to do with anything. Plenty of girls go to school—even Harriet did. We cannot all be like Mary, always educating ourselves. Some of us require motivation, and it is too bad Father never saw fit to give it, or I shouldn't be in the trouble I am now.

After returning from the spa yesterday, I went immediately to the library where, ignoring the assembled company, the tea, the coffee, and the fashionable periodicals, I made straight for the books and looked for the librarian. My courage almost failed me when he appeared. He looked so exactly as a librarian should, with his gray whiskers and faded brown coat and little spectacles on the end of his nose like Mary's—so very studious and learned. But my mission was urgent. I girded my loins.

"I should like to read the works of Saint Augustine," I said haughtily. "And I also need some poetry, novels, and plays."

"I see." The librarian frowned, and his spectacles slipped even farther down his nose. "Do you have anything more specific in mind?"

I crumbled.

"Nothing at all!" I cried. "I have just four days in which to become educated."

"How educated?" the librarian asked.

I slumped into a nearby armchair, feeling discouraged. There seemed no point in dissembling. "Just enough to be convincing," I admitted.

The librarian—who is a *charming* man—patted my shoulder, gave me Saint Augustine, and scurried away to gather a veritable tower of learning, the names of which I must write down to anchor them forever in my memory.

They were:

Jean-Jacques Rousseau, *The Social Contract*

William Shakespeare—*Hamlet, Richard III, Romeo and Juliet,* and the *Sonnets*

John Milton, *Paradise Lost*

Alexander Pope, *The Rape of the Lock*

Geoffrey Chaucer, *The Canterbury Tales*

"I have also included Mrs. Radcliffe's *The Mysteries of Udolpho*," he said. "I find a knowledge of contemporary culture is a very pleasing thing, and it is of course immensely fashionable."

"Of course." I gulped. "But all this—all this is what I have to read to appear intelligent?"

The librarian said, "Well, it's a start."

All those books! A *start*! I felt the blood drain from my face.

"If I may make a suggestion?" the librarian said gently.

"Please do," I whispered.

"It is not always necessary, to give an *impression* of learning, to have read entire works. As long as the conversation does not linger, selected chapters in many cases will suffice. The world does not expect young ladies to have read all of Mr. Rousseau. Or indeed, all of Saint Augustine. An introduction, an opening act, some judiciously chosen lines to quote at apposite moments . . . Would you like me to help you?"

I nodded. I had a lump in my throat. I don't think any stranger has been so nice to me, ever.

"You may settle in my private office, if you wish," he said. "You will not be disturbed there. And I shall prepare the books for you, and mark the appropriate pages, and explain what you do not understand. Perhaps you will develop a taste for learning— what a grand thing that would be!"

He opened a door, hidden among the stacks, revealing a

small room beyond. I saw a desk crowded with papers, a comfortable chair before the fireplace, a silver tray with a decanter of brandy, one wall that was not lined with books—it was exactly like Father's library at home. I had to bite my lip not to give way to proper tears.

"You had better send the books to my lodgings," I told him. "My friend—Mrs. Forster, I am staying with her—she would think it strange that I was come here to study. She is not accustomed to me reading—nobody is, really. I shall read the books quietly in my room, where it will not excite comment or suspicion. Pretend that I am ill, perhaps—yes, that is what I shall do. If you could mark them up, as you suggested, and be discreet when you send them. Pretend they are not books. Say—just say they are a delivery, and if anyone asks, pretend that they are clothes."

The librarian bowed. "As you wish," he said, but I could see that he was disappointed.

He showed me how to fill in a card with the titles of the books I wanted, and I gave him our Market Street address, and then he said the strangest thing as I left.

"Do not be afraid of books, Miss Bennet. Simply treat them with the respect they deserve, and you will be richly rewarded. You do not have to be clever or rich or have attended celebrated schools or universities in order to appreciate them. It is enough simply to have an open and receptive mind—and sometimes, it is true, a little perseverance. But you must not be afraid, Miss Bennet, for books do not judge you. Do you understand?"

I fled, clutching Saint Augustine to my bosom.

It has cost me five shillings—five shillings!—to subscribe to the library. The books arrived yesterday evening, and are stacked in a pile on the floor of my tiny bedroom. I can do this. They are only books, after all. How difficult can it be? How astonished Mary will be when she finds how learned I have become in Brighton! And Father, too! I shall make a great point when I go home of asking for a book to read from his library—not the novels Lizzy likes, with coaches driving off roads and maidens being rescued by pirates, but something serious and dull. That *will* be a joke! That will make them sit up!

But I have wasted enough time writing about this. To work, to work! For I have much to read before I see the Comte and Comtesse again.

WEDNESDAY, 24TH JUNE

I have done exactly as I said. I have feigned sickness, and spent the last four days in my room.

> *Long is the way and hard, that out of Hell leads up*
>   *to light.*
> *Hear and believe! Thy own importance know . . .*
> *Alas, poor Yorick!*
> *For hym was levere have at his beddes heed*
> *Twenty books, clad in blak or reed . . .*

The librarian was true to his word, and sent the books with notes on the most relevant pages, but even so my mind is fit to burst. No wonder Mary is always so cross. She must be constantly worried that her head is about to explode.

Harriet has seen the books, of course. It is impossible to hide anything in such a small house. I had to pretend I ordered them to stop myself being bored while I was ill. Wickham called this evening. I did not go down, but opened my door just an inch to hear what they were saying.

"*Reading*," Harriet said. "Real books. Shakespeare and poetry and something foreign."

"But Lydia never reads!" Wickham sounded astonished. "She is famous for it."

They all cackled unkindly. I closed the door softly.

It is all very well for Wickham to laugh, but I cannot recollect ever seeing *him* with a book in his hands. It is always cards with him, or a glass, or the reins of a horse. I bet he has never even heard of Saint Augustine or Milton. He probably hasn't even heard of *Shakespeare*.

He could never understand.

Books may not judge you, but people do.

THURSDAY, 25ᵀᴴ JUNE

J pretended I was ill again this morning, then waited until Harriet was gone before slipping out myself. I wore my newly tailored muslin—it seemed the safest option, since the Comtesse appeared to approve of it—but with white stockings this time instead of the "obvious" pantaloons, and my yellow straw bonnet. I shall never be as striking as she or as graceful as Lizzy—I may as well accept that right now—but I felt definitely as if I belonged more in Brighton than in Meryton.

I arrived at the Coach and Anchor at exactly eleven o'clock. The courtyard was crowded with all manner of people and contraptions and animals and luggage, all getting in each other's ways, but there was no sign of the Comte de Fombelle and his trap. Disappointment flooded me. He had not come—he *would* not come. They did not want me for a friend.

"Miss Bennet!"

A voice, strangely inflected but familiar. A blue frock coat pushing through the crowd, a tall hat at a jaunty angle over a head of black curls, that flash of scarlet from the scarf. He had come!

"I left the trap with a boy around the corner," he explained, as he offered me his arm. "The mayhem here! It reminds me of Madras."

"Oh, me too!" I had no idea what Madras was, but it seemed the right thing to say (I have since discovered it is a city in India).

A large woman elbowed past us, screeching after a footman.

"Actually, I take that back." He laughed. "Brighton is not nearly so calm."

I laughed, too, though I am still not sure why it was funny.

The Comte de Fombelle—Alaric—does not drive as fast as Wickham, but he is much more alarming, because he never looks where he is going and gets so involved in whatever he is talking about (he talks a *lot*) that he confuses the horse.

"What have you been doing, Miss Bennet, since last we saw you at the Chalybeate Spa? My sister says she did not spot you at the beach."

"Reading, mostly," I said. "I have . . . I have been a little unwell."

He expressed concern. Should he perhaps drive me home? Put off the expedition for another day? Tara was a little drive away, was I strong enough, was I sure? He pulled on the left rein as he turned to look at me. The horse ambled across the road.

I gently readjusted the reins. He didn't seem to notice. "I assure you I am feeling much better."

"Well, if you *assure* me, I shall have to believe you." I thought that he was teasing me, but then he said with great sincerity, "We are so pleased that you are come to visit. We are just returned from India these few weeks, you know, and we were children when we left, so we hardly know a soul, and we live so isolated up on the cliff top! You will have to tame us, Miss Bennet, and instruct us in proper English ways."

"Surely you have your aunt for that—Mrs. Lovett."

The Comte pulled a face. "She is perhaps a little *too* English and proper. She is very concerned with society, you know—appearances, and what people think." He smiled slyly. "That is the only reason she tolerates our wild ways, I think. She does not realize that beneath this noble exterior beats the heart of someone who wants to break free from society!"

"*Man is born free, and everywhere he is in chains . . .*" I murmured—delighted to be able to make such early use of my new reading.

"You've read Rousseau!" Alaric looked delighted. "How splendid! Do you know Voltaire as well?"

"I prefer Shakespeare," I said, trying not to panic.

"Me too! Theo laughs at me, and I suppose it is a little obvious—she detests all that is *obvious*—but there is nobody as good as Shakespeare in my opinion, nobody! I like the historical plays myself. *Richard III! Bad is the world; and all will come to naught, when such ill dealing must be seen in thought!*"

He dropped the reins, the better to wave his hands about as he declaimed. The gray mare wandered onto the verge to graze.

"So evil!" he cried. "And yet so human!"

"I think you had better see to the mare," I said, "before she tips us into the ditch."

"Greedy beast!" Alaric gathered the reins once more and cracked the whip, startling the mare into a canter that threw me back into my seat. "Thank heavens you are sensible as well as educated, Miss Bennet," he shouted. "Which play do *you* love most?"

"I like the sonnets," I said firmly. I had prepared for this. *"Shall I compare thee to a summer's day?"*

"Thou art more lovely and more temperate," Alaric cried above the clatter of hooves. *"Rough winds do shake the darling buds of May—"*

"And summer's lease hath all too short a date," I finished.

There was no need for me to quote more. The Comte de Fombelle recited the entire sonnet and two more besides by the time we reached the elephant-gated drive to Tara. The mare, which had slowed on the road up the hill, picked up speed again, sensing home. Overgrown meadows, grazing horses, and heavy trees passed in a blur and we clattered to a halt in a small stable yard, beside a shiny new carriage.

"Aunt Lovett's," the Comte said cheerfully. "She despises all forms of public transportation, and always takes her own. You saw her horses in the field."

He jumped down and held a hand up to me. I don't think he has a notion what a terrifying driver he is. "Let me just unhitch the mare, and then I'll take you down. You don't mind a bit of a walk, do you? It's easier than driving all the way to the house, for then I should have to bring her back again, and there is no one about to take care of her, apart from Aunt's coachman, but I don't like to ask him. Besides, I've grown fond of this beast, and it doesn't take a minute. He will help me put the trap away later."

Goodness, I thought as I watched him. I bet Mr. Darcy never sees to his own horse. That must be what it means to be of noble birth. They are above convention, and may do exactly as they please.

The mare, released from her harness, trotted amiably into the meadow to join the other horses. Alaric beamed, and offered me his arm. "Come!" he said. "And welcome to the most ridiculous house in England."

ᖇᘿᓑ

The driveway from the stables was short, winding through a tunnel of trees planted by Mr. John Shelton to protect it from the weather. "Except he didn't realize," the Comte de Fombelle explained, "that the wind would cause them to grow almost horizontal. They look quite mad, do not you think? Watch your footing, by the way. They have put out roots over the years, and it is easy to trip."

Together we walked below the gnarled canopy of trees, and even before I saw the house I had the strangest feeling that I was not at Brighton at all, or even in England, but in another land entirely, and that it was magic.

The tunnel opened onto a turning circle, a patchy lawn bordered by roses and grown over with wild chamomile, and beyond it—the most ridiculous house in England.

Except that it isn't.

The house is heaven. The house is *divine*. The house is exactly where I would like to live, forever and ever until I die.

Mr. Shelton, the Comte de Fombelle explained, built the house in the style of a South Indian palace. Its name is Indian, too—*Tara* means "star." It is white, and built on two stories, with carved pillars all along the front, and cornices that look like they might once have been gold, and three towers topped by strange onion-shaped domes, also gold. Tall windows at the front are protected by faded blue shutters, which are actually French, and were added by the Comte's mother to protect them from the constant whistling wind.

"It is a little shabby," the Comte said. "The house has been standing empty for so long, and has suffered from the weather. But we will soon put it right. When I was little, before we left for India, there were the most tremendous parties here. People used to come from miles around, and there was music and dancing, sometimes for days on end. Theo says we will do all that again, in time."

He pushed open the front door, which was made of heavy

wood, as intricately carved as the pillars. Inside, every room was a different color (downstairs, at least—I did not go upstairs). The vestibule is painted white and gold, and I glimpsed a sort of study on the left as we entered, red, with woodwork the same jade green as my earrings. The dining room is painted all over with a motif of peacock feathers, and the drawing room is the prettiest deep lilac, again with trims of gold, and all the stone floors are covered with Indian rugs and carpets, and everywhere there is the smell of incense, like church but nicer, and there is French lace at the windows, and screens painted with elephants and tigers.

Just as I thought it could not get any better, the Comte flung open the drawing-room windows, and we stepped out onto a stone terrace.

"The *pièce de résistance!*" he murmured, and there it was— the sea, at its bluest, most glorious, most extraordinary best, and we high above it like gulls, or eagles, or those boys who sit being lookouts at the top of the masts of tall, tall ships.

"It isn't bad," Alaric said with a smile. "For a ridiculous house."

It was so quiet there, so still and strangely beautiful—the exact opposite of plain, loud, always busy Longbourn. I could have stood there forever.

"Where is everybody?" I asked.

"Theo is in her workroom," he said. "And some neighbors came this morning for my aunt and Esther—they are gone shopping, I believe."

"And the servants?"

"There is only Marie, our housekeeper, who was *Maman*'s

maid, and came with her from France, and was with us in Madras, and has looked after us all our lives. Somewhere about are my aunt's maid and horseman, but they will go with her when she leaves."

"And that is all? Apart from Marie, you live *alone?*"

"Quite alone!" the Comte said cheerfully.

I gazed down at the sea, and then back toward the house. What heaven! I thought. To have your very own palace, and to live alone with no one to boss or nag or scold you . . .

"Come!" The Comte led me away from the terrace, down a narrow winding path bordered on either side with lavender, ending in a sheltered courtyard in which stood a miniature replica of Tara, colonnades and all.

"The summerhouse," the Comte announced. "Originally built as a folly for my mother, now taken over by Theo as a workroom. Ah, Patch has heard us—I can hear his barking."

He pushed open a wooden door as elaborately carved as that of the main house, and the little dog shot out, yapping and growling and leaping about us. The Comte gestured for me to enter, then followed me in with the dog in his arms furiously wriggling and licking his face.

Inside, the summerhouse consisted of only one plain room. None of the colors here like those of the big house, no rugs on the floor, no decorations or baubles. White walls and a stone floor swept clean, and a broom in the corner to ensure it remained so. A fireplace equally pristine, the only furniture a long table and two straight-backed chairs. But standing by the tall low windows, two dressmaker's manikins, the one swathed in cerulean blue muslin pinned with swatches of crimson stuff, the other sporting a bodice of the same green-and-white stripes as the Comtesse's dress from the other day, with the lady herself standing before it, carefully pinning orange piping about the ruched sleeves.

She glanced up as we entered. Today she wore a severe dress of navy blue, with a white fichu beneath a calico apron, and spectacles perched precariously on the end of her nose. ("Her dressmaking outfit," the Comte whispered. "And the spectacles are purely for show.")

"What do you think of this orange?" she asked by way of greeting. "I like bold patterns and colors, but I don't think it is quite right."

I did not know what to say, but I don't think she expected an answer.

Her workroom was like a treasure cave. Bolts of cloth such as I have never seen lay stacked on shelves built into the alcoves by the fireplace—plain muslins the colors of precious jewels, checked cottons, striped satins and silks, all brought over from India. On the table were several wooden trays inlaid with mother-of-pearl on which, neatly arranged, lay pins and needles, thimbles and scissors, and all the tools of the dressmaker's trade, and a great pile of *La Belle Assemblée* (infinitely more appealing than my library books). A giant board leaned against a wall, to which were pinned a multitude of drawings, quite as good as any you see in the fashion periodicals, but outlandish and exciting, too, using the patterns and fabrics from her collection—evening gowns and walking dresses, short jackets, long coats, clothes for children, for men, for women.

"All hers," Alaric said with a proud look.

I crossed the room to examine them.

"This one." I pointed at a drawing of a three-quarter-length pelisse, a sprigged brown-and-green oak leaf motif, with a lining of leopard fur. "This is the one I like the best."

It is quite hard to describe the Comtesse de Fombelle looking pleased. It involves a sort of pursing of the lips, which makes most people look pinched, but in her I think is an attempt to disguise a smile. She said that it was her favorite, too, but that she could not make it yet, on account of not having any leopard fur.

"One day!" she said. "Now, what sort of dress would you like?"

"I beg your pardon?"

"That is why you are here, is it not? For me to make you a dress?"

"Why yes, of course. That is to say . . ." Was it? Had I agreed to her making me a dress? I could not remember, but did not want to offend. And if I did agree, was I supposed to pay her? How much? What with the parasol and ostrich feather and pantaloons, my small allowance from Mamma is already severely depleted.

The Comtesse was frowning as her brother whispered in her ear. "Oh, very well," I heard her say, and then she turned toward me.

"My dear Miss Bennet, I should like to make you a gift of a

dress. No, no, do not thank me. I am making one for my cousin as well. The first dress ball of the season is on the sixteenth of July, and it is a terribly grand affair. Dressed by me, you shall be the most elegant, exquisite creatures in the room. I shall make you look like a princess. No, a queen! There, Alaric! Was not that prettily expressed?"

She glared at her brother. I had the feeling the offer to make me a dress for nothing came from him. A part of me felt mortified, knowing that he had guessed me to be short of funds, and wanted to refuse. Another part of me thought . . . well, a new dress!

"Quite prettily." Alaric smiled. "Though you have some distance to go before you are truly polite. And I do not believe the offer to be entirely devoid of interest, for Miss Bennet will be an excellent advertisement for your business."

"She shall, shall she not? Look at her, Ally! Tall, and that excellent, robust English complexion, that firm bosom, and those strong shoulders . . . She is the exact opposite of Esther."

I blushed. The Comtesse grabbed a measuring tape. "Stand still while I measure you," she ordered.

But the Comte took the tape out of her hands. "Another day, Theo. I believe we invited Miss Bennet for luncheon. If she agrees to your proposition, I shall fetch her from town again another day. Or you could go to her, you know. I believe that is also how these things are done."

His sister arched her eyebrows at me. "Well?" she said. "You have not said a word. Shall I make you a dress?"

"Yes, please," I cried. "And I would far sooner come back here. When should I return?"

The Comtesse waved a vague but gracious hand and said, "Whenever you wish."

Alaric proclaimed himself delighted, and we repaired to the main house for luncheon, where to my relief there was no need to discuss literature or indeed anything else, for the Comtesse dominated the table entirely with her talk of clothes. The Comte told me on the drive home that she plans to make a profession of her dressmaking. I can't think why. A profession sounds like monstrous hard work, and for what? But I am not complaining. After all, *I* am to have a dress made for me by a countess!

THURSDAY, 2ND JULY

A whole week has passed, in which *nothing* has happened. "Whenever you wish," the Comtesse said— but how was I to get there? She didn't offer to send the trap for me, and I can't very well write and ask. A hackney all the way out there would be too expensive, and I refuse to ask Harriet for help. She would only want to come, too, and take everything over. I hoped I might see the Comtesse at the beach, but she has not come at all. It has been extremely vexing. But then this morning Wickham called, as Harriet and I were changing in our rooms after returning from our bathe.

Harriet, whose hair becomes uncontrollably frizzy after she

has been in the sea, said that she could not possibly show herself in such a state, and I should go down and entertain him alone.

"I came to see how you were," he said as I entered the room. "I heard you were afflicted by a sudden love of reading."

"Very funny," I said, and would have ignored him, when it dawned on me how he could help.

"Do you still have Denny's curricle?" I asked.

"I do," he replied. "Poor Denny just keeps on losing."

"Harriet!" I shouted up the stairs. "Wickham is going to accompany me to Munro's to look at their new gloves."

I pushed him out of the house before she could come down.

"Gloves?" Wickham queried.

"It's all I could think of. I actually need you to drive me to Tara. They have invited me," I could not resist adding.

Suddenly, Wickham looked interested. "So the spa plan worked, did it? Well done, Lydia! I am excessively impressed. How did you do it?"

"I don't think I should go into details," I said primly.

Wickham grinned. "I don't suppose the reading disease has anything to do with this new friendship?"

"Oh, you are impossible!"

We had arrived at the library. I dropped his arm and we stood facing each other, I annoyed, he curious.

"Very well." He smiled. "I will take you."

"Thank you!"

He strolled away to fetch the curricle from the stables where Denny keeps it. I sat on a bench outside the library to wait. It was very pleasant to sit in the sun watching people come and go, but as Wickham returned I was struck by a terrible thought.

"Will my dress do?" I asked. I was wearing my green spotted muslin. "It is just an old thing—I did not think, when I changed after bathing, that I would be going to Tara."

Wickham looked me slowly up and down. "You'll do," he said, and I had to make a great fuss of climbing into the curricle so he would not see me blush. He is such an irritating man! I asked him to leave me at the elephant gate, and he laughed at me. "I understand. Your old friends do not suit your new high-flown connections!"

"Oh, go away!"

It took ages to walk to Tara from the road. I was hot and thirsty by the time I reached the house, but there was nobody about. Too late, I realized the folly of rushing out here without a proper appointment, or knowing how I should return! But the front door swung open when I pushed it, and so I tiptoed in. I walked through the white-and-gold hall with its black-and-white floor tiles, and into the lilac drawing room. It was empty. I crossed to look at the view from the window, then turned to the piano-forte, which was open, with a stack of sheet music and a bowl of freshly arranged flowers on top. Suddenly, I wished more than anything that I knew how to play. Why did I never pursue lessons, like Lizzy and Mary? Lizzy is right—I *am* idle. I fingered a key, then another, and another. In my head, more notes poured out, rushing one after the other to become great concertos. A room of enraptured spectators sat upon rows of chairs as I played.

The Comte de Fombelle stood at the back, smiling at me . . . *There used to be such parties here . . .*

"Who are you?" I jumped as a woman's voice cut into my daydream. Mrs. Lovett stood in the doorway, regarding me with suspicion.

Mrs. Lovett dresses expensively, but you can tell that *she* is not French, nor a person of rank. There is something too fussy about her clothes that reminds me of Harriet.

I curtsied. "I am Lydia Bennet."

"Are you a friend of my niece's?"

"Not exactly . . . I am come about a dress."

"Oh, goodness, *that*." She exhaled sharply. I have the impression she is not much impressed by the Comtesse's eccentric career notions.

"You are staying in town?"

"Yes, ma'am. With Colonel Forster, of the Derbyshire militia."

"Oh, the militia." She sniffed. I get the feeling she disapproves of them just as much as she does of her stepniece's dressmaking. "Well, we must all stay somewhere. I'm afraid Théodorine and my daughter are not at home. They went out in the trap, quite unaccompanied. I don't know what the world is coming to. And now I am going out, and cannot very well leave you alone. You had better return to Brighton with me, and come again tomorrow."

"But I am very happy to wait . . ."

"I will look after Miss Bennet." My heart leaped as the

Comte de Fombelle appeared in the doorway, wearing a banyan over his trousers and shirt, a stick of drawing charcoal in his hand. He looked marvelous—an Indian banyan is so much more stylish than an English dressing gown—but Mrs. Lovett frowned again, doubtless thinking his attire unsuitable. "She and I are old friends. Go to your engagement, dear Aunt, and I shall look after her as best I can until Theo and Esther return."

Mrs. Lovett finally departed, after much protesting on her part about how improper it was to leave us together, and much assurance on the Comte's that his sister and cousin would return shortly, that the housekeeper Marie was in the kitchen and that I would be very happy playing the pianoforte until his sister and cousin returned.

"Thank goodness for that," he said with a smile as we heard the sound of the carriage departing. "Come, never mind the instrument. Let me show you my study. You'll see that Theo isn't the only one here with an empire."

Goodness, how the Comte de Fombelle talks! My brain was bursting by the time we reached his study. We made slow progress getting there, because it is right at the top of the house and he kept stopping every few steps the better to tell his story, of how he and his sister and their mother first arrived in England after fleeing the Revolution, how they lived for a year in a tiny cottage because the revolutionaries had taken all their money as well as their castle in Normandy, how Mr. John Shelton had fallen in love with their *maman* at first sight because she was so good and beautiful, and married her, and brought them all to live here—it had seemed like a fairy-tale house to them, and although his sister had always adored the summerhouse, *he* had a special fondness for the attic room where he was taking me now.

"It feels like a fairy-tale house to me, too," I told him. He beamed, and said he was glad to hear it, and walked up a few more steps, then stopped again to tell how their stepfather grew homesick for India. "So off we went again, to the heat and dust, and it was even more wonderful than here," but even so he never forgot the miniature Indian palace high on the cliff and the room at the top of the house, and when they had to leave India he told himself that he would go straight there and make it his own.

"And here it is!"

Finally, we had reached the top of the stairs, and stood upon a narrow landing. The Comte threw open a door, and I stepped into his study.

It is one long gallery, the length of the whole house, the coziest place you can imagine, with a sofa and armchairs gathered about a fireplace, and a vast painting of an Indian palace above it, and a great collection of the strangest statues I ever saw upon the mantel, of people with eight arms and snake bodies and elephant heads. The outside wall was almost entirely hidden by prints of houses, both Indian and English, and at the far end of the room was an elevated table covered in papers and drawing materials, with rolls of paper stacked on shelves beside it.

"Architectural drawings," the Comte explained. "Architecture is my passion—like dressmaking for Theo. I hope one day to make it my profession."

I forced a smile, but inside my heart was faltering—for all the wall space that was not covered in drawings was taken up by books.

"Are you quite well?" Alaric asked.

I scarcely had the strength to answer—had he actually read them all?

The sound of footsteps on the stairs forced me to rally. A female voice called "Al! Alaric! Are you up there?" The footsteps drew nearer, the door flew open, and the Comtesse de Fombelle burst into the room in her emerald silk beach dress, damp hair tumbling down her back, and her hemline quite white with salt.

"Miss Bennet!" She glanced sharply from me to her brother. "This is a surprise."

"I came about the dress," I said. "I'm sorry, I should have sent a note. A friend was driving out this way, and offered to bring me."

"Well, then you had better come with me," she replied. "My cousin Esther is downstairs. You can sit with her while I change."

೧ﮩ๑

Esther Lovett is exactly the sort of person Lizzy would approve of. She is *tremendously* accomplished. She was playing something complicated on the piano when the Comtesse and I came down from the Comte's study, she speaks French with the Comtesse, and one of her watercolors sits upon the mantelpiece. She has also read every single one of Shakespeare's sonnets. I know, because it was almost the first thing she said to me. "Alaric says you like Shakespeare. I am so glad. I have read every one of his sonnets."

The Comtesse left us alone for some ten minutes, then swept back into the room in her navy-blue dressmaking outfit, and ushered us out to the summerhouse. "Since I am making Esther a dress for the ball as well, there is a lot to do, and not a minute to lose."

It is very impressive to watch her work, and a little terrifying. She frowned a great deal as she took my measurements, and demanded silence as she wrote them down, and then she rummaged through her stack of cloths and jabbed me several times as she pinned various samples to me. She would not let me choose the fabric for my dress. My heart settled on a luscious lavender silk, but she said that she would decide on everything, and please could I not move. And so I tried not to talk or fidget, and to stand as still and silent as possible, and imagined what it must be like to be a woman with a profession. Would there be magazine articles about her creations, such as we read in the fashion periodicals at home? Imagine perfect strangers talking about something you have made—not just in Meryton or Brighton, but farther afield—in London, or in Paris! I should like that, I think. Yes, I should like that very much.

Afterward, over a simple lunch, the Comtesse interrogated me much as her aunt had, without letting anyone else get a word in. Where did I come from? Where was I staying? Colonel Forster? The Derbyshire militia? What sort of people were they?

"Theo, for heaven's sake," her brother remonstrated. "Leave

poor Miss Bennet alone. Esther, talk to her about books or plays or something. Theo should be forbidden from ever making conversation, if she is going to ask such dull questions."

I saw what he was trying to do—stop his sister from haranguing me. It was kindly meant, but I wished he hadn't, for if there was one thing worse than being interrogated by the Comtesse, surely it must be discussing literature with Miss Lovett. But Miss Lovett had unaccountably spilled her wine all over the tablecloth, and was covered in confusion. The Comte leaned forward to help her.

"Well, and are you fond of the theater, Miss Bennet?" he asked as he dabbed away at the cloth with his table napkin.

"Monstrous fond!" I cried, wildly wondering what I should say next. "Why, I was lucky enough to go just the other day!"

"What was the play?"

I told him. I thought I saw the Comtesse smirk. I suppose *The Weathercock* is not refined enough for her, but luckily her brother is not so superior, and kept up a cheerful stream of chatter, first demanding details of the production and then not listening to my answers as he recounted *his* last visit to the theater, in London, before coming to Brighton.

"I will lend it to you," he said. "I have it upstairs. You can tell me what you think of it next time we meet."

"Oh yes, do read it," Theo said as he rushed away to fetch the book. "I'm sure we would all be fascinated to hear your thoughts."

Was she laughing at me? Has she guessed? I was all confusion and embarrassment as Alaric re-entered the room, and I am quite sure everybody saw.

"You must not mind Theo," Alaric assured me again as he drove me home. "Since our mother died, she has become some-what authoritarian, but she means well."

"I do not think she likes me very much."

"Why, she is making you a dress! And not demanding pay-ment for it—that is a great concession for her, you know. She says she will only do it for friends."

"She is making it because you asked her to."

He colored slightly at that, and I did not pursue the conver-sation further, but I smiled to myself inside.

The Comtesse de Fombelle may not like me, but her brother does.

Harriet was annoyed again when I came home, and asked where I had been. "I went to the library after Munro's," I told her, waving Alaric's book. "I was so engrossed, I did not see the time." I think she believed me, and no wonder, with that great pile of books all over my floor. And now I have *another* book to read. *Macbeth*—more dreary Shakespeare! It sits on my bed, glaring at me. Oh dear, Alaric's library! However much I try to read, I don't suppose that I shall ever catch up. Well, I am not going to think about that now—or read any more books tonight. I will write a long letter to my sisters instead, and tell them about my new dress.

FRIDAY, 3ᴿᴰ JULY

I was right to worry that Wickham has no intention of honoring the promise he made to me on my birthday.

He called again just after breakfast. "You again!" Harriet said with a sniff. "If you are come to take Lydia for another of your drives, I shan't allow it. And you are not to allow her to wander off to that library, either. She brought another book home yesterday!"

"Just a short walk by the sea," Wickham said, and pushed me out of the cottage before Harriet could object.

It was lovely, at first. Wickham tucked my hand in his arm, and as we walked toward the sea, he told me a long silly story about an argument between Carter and Pratt over a racing bet.

He was so easy and amiable I thought how delightful it was to be taking a stroll on a sunny day with a handsome officer in a smart uniform, talking of this and that and knowing that all the disapproving looks we got concealed hearts absolutely green with envy. We turned right when we reached East Cliff and began to walk away from town. Gradually, the crowds thinned, and we were quite alone—and everything changed.

"Tell me, how was your visit yesterday?"

"Most excellent," I said, and proceeded to tell him all about it.

"And so they are grown very fond of you, are they?"

"Monstrous fond!" I boasted.

"I wonder," he said, "if you could introduce me to Miss Lovett."

I gasped. I honestly felt as though he had slapped me.

"But you promised!" I stammered.

"What exactly did I promise?"

"That you would not . . ." I tried to remember. "That you would not pursue rich young women, or try to ruin them."

"I have no intention of ruining Miss Lovett."

"But you mean to pursue her."

"I mean to *marry* her," he corrected.

Wickham's teeth are very pointed. I never noticed before today. Sometimes, when he smiles, they make him look exactly like a wolf.

"I hardly know her," I said.

"Oh, *that* doesn't matter! No one ever knows anyone in a

place like Brighton, and yet everyone is bosom friends—people who wouldn't be seen dead together in other circumstances!"

"And she is all wrong for you, Wickham! She is no fun at all, you know. She is polite and quiet and accomplished and . . ."

And she spills her wine at the mention of the Derbyshire militia.

I remembered the first time we saw her, at the card party at the Ship Assembly Rooms—the expression on her face as she gazed across at Wickham. Oh God—it was too late—she had already fallen! Esther Lovett, with her mild manners, and her mousy looks . . . If Wickham is a wolf, she is a lamb to the slaughter.

"You mustn't," I said. "And I won't."

Wickham said nothing—only waited.

"She is all wrong!" I repeated desperately. "She speaks French, and paints watercolors, and recites Shakespeare . . ."

"Ah," he said. "Shakespeare."

I knew then he would do something awful. I bit my lip, waiting to hear what it would be.

"I wonder," Wickham said thoughtfully, "how the Comte and Comtesse de Fombelle would feel, knowing how their new friend has lied to secure their affections."

"Lied?"

"The books, Lydia! Shakespeare, Saint Augustine . . ."

"How do you know what I'm reading?"

He smiled, pulled a coin from his pocket. Tossed it in the air, caught it, held it up so it glinted in the light.

"Maids talk."

"You bribed Sally!"

"A useful ally," he agreed. "So, Lydia. What do you say? What would your new friends think, if they knew your reading was all for show?"

At home at Longbourn, the farm boy has this way of catching rabbits. He knows where all the warrens are, and he blocks all the entrances off with thorns and brambles, all except one. Then he sits there by the one unblocked entrance with his gun and his terrier Mabel, and kills them as they come out. People tease him about how long he's prepared to wait, and Hill even once bought him a ferret from a peddler, but he just says the rabbits always come out in the end, and you've just got to be prepared to wait.

I felt exactly like those rabbits today.

"I ask only for an introduction," Wickham said.

"You don't even know them," I told him. "You couldn't tell them. You *wouldn't*."

But I knew that he could, and would.

Longbourn,
July 2nd

Dear Lydia,

Mary says I have to write to you. She says she
understands that I was friends with Harriet
first and that you behaved very ill in making
her invite you instead of me, but that I have to
forgive you, just as Jesus forgave the Romans
who nailed him to the Cross. If Jesus can
forgive that, Mary says, I must be able to
forgive you, but I bet if Jesus had wanted to
go to Brighton, he would have. He would have
walked right over the water from Galilee and
had a lovely time, and I am sure it would have
made all that came afterward much easier to
bear. I told Mary as much. "Explain to me why
I should forgive her," I said, "when she has
stolen my friend and my happiness and is
probably getting a husband as we speak."

    I am not very sure what it means,
anyway, to forgive. If it means I hope you
are enjoying yourself, I suppose I do. It
would be an awful waste, for you to have been
so nasty and selfish and <u>not</u> have a good
time. Everyone else is vastly dull. Jane is still
mooning over Mr. Bingley, and I don't

know what is come over Lizzy, but she also spends a monstrous amount of time drooping about and sighing. By the way, I wish you would buy me a parasol like the one you described. I should like mine to be a different color from yours, though, so people do not say I have copied you. And no bows, please. I have an abhorrence of bows, ever since Maria started wearing them on everything, because her London cousin told her they were fashionable.

There, I have done it and shown Mary the letter. She says that it is not exactly what she had in mind, but that it is a start. She is in a foul temper because she is learning German and wants Father to send her to Heidelberg. She says, "If Lydia can go to Brighton to buy umbrellas, why can I not go to Heidelberg to improve my mind?" but he says who would accompany her and a woman may not travel alone, especially through France, with all those soldiers about. She says she is going to run away, but I do not believe her.

Your forgiving sister,
Kitty Bennet

PS: I must say, you are very mysterious. What is this great secret you can't tell me about? And are you actually in love with Wickham? Because you do write about him an awful lot.

PPS: Hill says that all the she-cats for two miles around are pregnant. She says that it is all Napoleon's fault, and that we should drown the kittens. Father says we should drown Napoleon, too.

SATURDAY, 4TH JULY

For a moment, reading Kitty's letter, I wished I could be home at Longbourn, where everything is boring but simple and there is little risk of finding yourself blackmailed by unprincipled pirate types you keep thinking are your friends but who turn out to be scoundrels.

I thought about them all night—Esther Lovett, the Comte, the Comtesse. It's not true that I want to go home. More than anything, I want to be here, I mean *there*—at Tara, with them. But I could not do it. I *would* not do it. I would not expose Esther Lovett to Wickham, and if it meant Wickham exposing me to them, then so be it. I would not be a party to his scheming—he says he wants to marry her, but I know what *that* means. I daresay he wanted to marry Georgiana Darcy, too, but unlike him, I have principles.

I felt very proud of myself for being so noble, but this morning there was a knock on the door, and the Comtesse de Fombelle stood on our step in her green dress and yellow jacket wearing a gentleman's top hat adorned with a matching swathe of canary gauze. Harriet's jaw dropped so far it practically nestled in her cleavage.

"Er . . . this is the Comtesse de Fombelle," I said. "We met, um, at the spa. Comtesse, this is Mrs. Forster."

"Delighted, delighted!" Harriet gushed, obviously torn between admiration of a title and astonishment at that title's outfit. "What an . . . interesting hat!"

"Thank you. It is my brother's. What a . . . charming cottage." The Comtesse quickly ran out of small talk. "I am come to take Miss Bennet for a drive," she declared.

"A drive!" Harriet is become so entirely transparent to me now, I could tell what she was thinking. *A drive! With a countess! What an honor! What reflected glory upon me! But how does Lydia know her? And yet, why should Lydia have all the fun? Why should not I go, too? And how does she make emerald and canary look so stylish, and could I carry off a top hat?*

The Comtesse—who may or may not also be a mind reader—did not extend her invitation, but said we had to leave *now*.

"I will fetch my coat and hat," I said.

"We may bathe," she whispered, and I ran from the room to hide my grin.

She does like me! That was all that I could think. She likes me! She was waiting for me outside, in the small black trap.

"I trust you have no objection to being driven by a woman, Miss Bennet?"

"I do not!"

"Then step aboard, and let us go!"

∽✑↷

Theo (that is how I think of her, though I daren't call her so to her face) drives better than Alaric, but the journey was not so comfortable as with her brother. She did not declaim poetry while the mare meandered along the verges, and I knew better than to try to impress her. We neither of us spoke much until we passed the entrance to Tara, when I asked where we were going.

"You will see!" she cried. Suddenly, she was in great high spirits. She clicked her tongue, and the mare broke into a brisk trot.

We stopped at the very cove I had looked at with Wickham, the one with the sparkling sapphire water. Theo climbed down from the trap, tied the mare to a tree, and signaled for me to follow her down a narrow path to the beach.

"One of the first rules of swimming in open water, Miss Bennet," she explained. "You may not undertake it alone. Alaric refuses to swim in this country because he says the water is too cold, and Esther, bless her, is too much of a goose. But my brother was sure you would be game. Are you?"

"Indeed I am!" I shouted, swallowing my fear.

216

"How I do detest those absurd bathing machines!" she continued. "And yet I must swim. You are about to taste a little bit of paradise, Miss Bennet. And please don't think that it is improper, for the road is hardly used, and anyhow you can barely see the beach unless you come right up to the edge of the cliff."

The day was warm, the tide low. We changed into our shifts out in the open, with no fuss or jolting about, and the wind on my bare skin felt delicious.

"Are you afraid?" she asked as we walked down to the water.

"I am never afraid," I lied, even though my heart was thumping at the sight of all that open water. Swimming unassisted in the open sea! Janet never prepared me for this!

We picked our way over dry stones and pebbles. The beach turned to fine shingle at the water's edge, and I gasped as the cold water lapped my toes. Going into the water little by little is very different from jumping off the steps of a bathing machine. It is much more difficult and yet at the same time infinitely more delicious.

"I am a very new swimmer," it finally occurred to me to inform her.

The Comtesse said it did not matter.

"What you must do," she said as we stood up to our knees in the sea, with our arms spread out to the sides, and our hands beating the water, "is wait for a good-sized wave and dive straight underneath it just as it begins to break."

"I am rather new to diving, too," I admitted.

A wave broke. "Just watch me!" she shouted, and plunged beneath it.

She re-emerged beyond the breaking waves and began to swim parallel to the beach while I splashed about in the shallows. At first, I only jumped over the smaller waves, or fell backward into the frothing foam. Then a larger wave knocked me off my feet. For a few terrifying seconds, I flailed about in tumbling water, until I remembered Janet's instructions and stamped my foot on the seabed. I shot back to the surface, realizing to my surprise that the water came only as high as my thighs. From then on there was no stopping me, and I threw myself into the waves with abandon. I even taught myself to dive beneath them, as Theo had, and she was right—it was paradise.

The Comtesse returned from her swim, and we lay side by side at the water's edge. The wind raised goose pimples all over my body as it blew against my wet shift, and the sun burned my face and arms and legs, and the sea dug grooves and channels all about my body as it rushed in and out around me. I tipped my head back so that it rested in the sand, and stared at the gulls circling in the cloudless sky, and in my head I laughed and laughed and laughed, because this was me, on a beach with a countess a million miles from Meryton.

When we grew too cold, we left the water and lay upon the hot stones to dry.

"I would love to swim like you," I said with a sigh.

"Mr. Lovett—our stepfather, you know, and Esther's uncle—believes that every person should know how to swim. It was he who taught us. There are miles of beaches in India. We used to ride out with him and *Maman* along the sand, and bathe wherever he deemed it safe."

"He sounds wonderful," I exclaimed.

"He has his moments," she said.

"I nearly drowned once, trying to swim in our stream. A farmhand rescued me and brought me home, and my father hit me."

"My stepfather struck me, too," Theo said thoughtfully. "I found a snake in our garden—beautiful, patterned, with a hooded head. It was a cobra, and it was dead—but my brother did not know. He ran crying to Mr. Shelton, thinking that I would die, and Mr. Shelton hurled the snake into the bushes and smacked me."

She rubbed her cheek as she spoke, possibly where Mr. Shelton had struck her. She was lying on her side, and her shift had ridden up, showing off her long bare legs, and she had raked her fingers through her hair and spread it about her shoulders to dry.

Lying there next to her felt like being with one of my sisters.

"We do what we must for the people we love, even if we hurt them," she said. "I think, Miss Bennet, that your father did not beat you because you tried to swim. I think he beat you because you nearly drowned, and he could not bear to lose you."

It was a remarkable thought. I pondered it for a while in silence.

"May I ask you a question?" I said at last.

"That rather depends on the question."

"Why do you talk of wanting a profession?"

She was silent, too, then sighed, and began to pull her dress on straight over her shift. I dressed, too, worried that I had offended her, but eventually she spoke.

"When we came over from France," she said, "we had nothing. Our home was confiscated, our father was dead, our mother was able to smuggle only a few pieces of jewelry she sold for a pittance when we arrived, barely enough to rent a small cottage. So she worked. She was a talented seamstress—she taught me everything I know—and she took in sewing. She began to work for old Mr. Shelton—my stepfather's father, who was a tailor. I used to watch her as she sewed. I saw how her neck hurt from continually bending over, how tired her eyes were from working in dim light, how her head ached, but I saw, too, how clever she was, and how much better than he, though she was never credited for her work, and how he grew rich while we remained poor. Those were hard times, Miss Bennet. Exiled, bereaved, with no money and no future . . ."

"But then she met Mr. John Shelton."

"Indeed. My stepfather met her when he returned from India, and she came to his father's shop to deliver a dress. He is . . . he is a passionate man, given to grand gestures. He fell violently in love with my mother and married her within six weeks of their meeting. And so we were elevated out of poverty, and into a new life. But even as a girl, I made myself two promises."

"What were they?"

"I promised myself that we would never be poor again, and

220

that one day, I would show the world that a woman can be as good in business as any man. I don't mean to be just a seamstress, Miss Bennet. I intend my drawings to be published, and to become a person of influence."

We had been walking up from the cove as she spoke, and now stood on top of the cliff. Theo frowned as she looked back down at the beach.

"Alaric is three years younger than me—too young to remember any of this. He has a romantic notion that we were happy in our poverty. He is more carefree than I. He believes that life will always come out well, but he is not a fighter, like me. It falls upon me to protect him. Do you understand?"

I did not, but I nodded anyway, and she appeared satisfied. I had hoped that we would stop at Tara on the way home, but she said that Alaric was not well, and could not receive visitors. She set me down again near the library.

"Thank you for accompanying me today, Miss Bennet," she said. "I have not enjoyed such a swim for a long time, and I was impressed by your prowess in the water."

"I was rather impressed myself," I admitted.

She drove away, calling out that we would meet again soon, and I watched her go, warm with the feeling that, contrary to all early indications, the Comtesse Théodorine de Fombelle might actually like me. The way she lay there on the beach—as easy and natural as if she had been my sister! The confidences we shared! I have never had a friend like her.

It was only once she had gone, and I had returned to our

lodgings where Harriet told me somewhat grumpily Wickham had called again while I was out, that I thought again about Esther Lovett and my promise to him.

How can I be close to Alaric and Theo, if I am betraying them behind their backs by helping Wickham meet Miss Lovett? And yet how can they know the truth, when I have lied to them so convincingly? This is my chance—my one chance. And it isn't so very much to ask, is it? An introduction?

Wickham is Wickham—he will break promises, and he will do whatever it takes to advance himself, and he will not give up.

If I don't do it, somebody else will.

Longbourn
Wednesday, 8th July

Dear Lydia,

How happy your last letter made us! We are so thrilled
for you, my pet! To think, that you should have a dress
made for you by French nobility! Infinitely preferable,
I am sure, to having a dress made by an English lady,
because in fashion the French, for all their faults, are
still superior to us, I think, and your aunt Philips
agrees. And to think you are so very friendly with them!
I am not surprised. With her good looks and amiable
nature, my Lydia makes friends wherever she goes! You
must let us know, dear, if there is anything at all you
need. I am sure you are being a credit to your family.

        Send my regards to Mrs. Forster, and to the Colonel,
and Denny and Carter and dear Wickham. How lonely we
are without them! And now Lizzy is gone away with your
aunt and uncle. She was to go to the Lakes but your uncle
must return to town earlier than planned, and so they are
gone into Derbyshire, and the house is very empty.

                        Ever your loving
                        Mamma

THURSDAY, 9ᵀᴴ JULY

"*T*here is to be a public reading tomorrow afternoon," Wickham told me the Sunday after our walk. "It will take place at the library. The eminent novelist Mrs. Radcliffe is to come and read from her books. I have it from Mrs. Lovett's maid that Miss Lovett is an ardent admirer—*Udolpho* is her favorite book, and it is a rare treat, for Mrs. Radcliffe rarely appears in public. The entire Tara party will be attending, with the possible exception of the Count, who is being kept home by his sister on account of a cold. You and I shall also attend, though separately. You will arrive early, and find a way to sit with your new friends. At some point in the evening's proceedings, I shall contrive to cross your path. You shall return my greeting, and, as is only right and proper, you will introduce me to Miss Lovett. That is all I ask."

"The Comte de Fombelle is still ill? I hope it is nothing serious!" How awful, if his illness should prevent me from returning to Tara!

"Lydia!" I forced my attention back to Wickham. "You do remember our arrangement, don't you?"

"You will tell the Comte de Fombelle I have been lying," I grumbled. "Yes, I remember, and I hate you."

Of all the books the librarian gave me to read, Mrs. Radcliffe's *The Mysteries of Udolpho* is the only one that is actually readable— all castles and ghosts and Italian brigands. I was a little surprised that Esther should like it so much too, but as we approached the library on Monday it seemed that the whole of Brighton shared her admiration for its author, because by the time I arrived with Harriet and Mrs. Conway, the library was almost as crowded as the theater had been, with seats laid out in rows before a small platform, on which stood a small table and chair. I glanced anxiously about me. Wickham was already there, standing where he could survey proceedings from the back of the room.

Even then, I told myself I would not do as he asked. I would *not* sit with the party from Tara, and I would *not* introduce him. They entered. Mrs. Lovett was dressed as usual like Mamma, in an old-fashioned dress and fichu, Esther Lovett in washed-out lavender, the Comtesse in the cerulean-blue muslin I had seen in progress in her workroom, with red piping about her short military jacket, a ruff of lace at her throat, and a blue hat with a black veil, piled high with cherries, netting, and a small stuffed bird.

"Goodness," Harriet tittered. "How extraordinary your countess looks, Lydia."

"*Is* she a countess?" Mrs. Conway peered through her lorgnette. "She looks more like a music hall singer."

"I think she's perfectly splendid," I retorted.

"She is making Lydia a dress," Harriet confided.

"Making Lydia a dress!" exclaimed Mrs. Conway. "How very droll! I do hope, Lydia, she shall exercise some reserve when it comes to dressing *you*. It is all very well drawing attention to herself if she wants to, but quite another to expose young ladies . . ."

"Will you excuse me?"

I could not stay with them a moment longer, but made my way through the crowd to the Comtesse and her party. For all their poisonous gossip, I did not miss the jealous look that passed between Harriet and her friend when the Comtesse and Miss Lovett indicated an empty seat beside them.

Maybe I would sit with them, then.

But I would not introduce Wickham.

The librarian took to the stage, whiskers twitching, spectacles gleaming, his whole body quivering with excitement. I remembered how warmly he had spoken of Mrs. Radcliffe at our first meeting, and forgot my worries for a moment in feeling pleased for him: His introduction over, he stepped aside for the lady herself to take her place. The room burst into spontaneous, rapturous applause, and I must confess, for the duration of the reading, I was myself quite entranced. She is not at all as I imagine a bookish person to be. She is very small and pretty and well dressed, and her voice as she read was warm, and her story was thrilling—infinitely better than Shakespeare or Saint Augustine. If books were all like hers, I would read much more. The reading finished. Immediately, spectators leaped from their seats to form a queue before Mrs. Radcliffe's table. "What are they doing?" I asked Miss Lovett, who had also leaped to her feet.

"It is a signing queue," she responded. "They are come to ask her to sign her books. Look, I have brought my own copy of *Udolpho*, which I take everywhere. And I mean to buy a copy of *The Italian*, and have her sign that for me, too. But oh! Look how long the purchasing queue is! They shall be all gone, if we do not hurry."

And although it pains me to write it, Wickham really is something of a genius. He arrived, as I knew he would, and I introduced him, as I knew I would have to. Theo and Mrs. Lovett curtsied very correctly. Miss Lovett blushed to the roots of her hair and tripped over her feet. And then, perceiving her distress at the length of the purchasing queue . . .

"I have myself acquired two copies of her books," Wickham said, producing them from his coat pocket, one of them being *The Italian*. "Perhaps the young ladies would do me the honor of accepting them?"

The young ladies did. Theo took hers like a queen accepting homage. I thought Miss Lovett might die of suffocation.

They insisted on reimbursing him before rushing off to have the books signed. He would not hear of it. *Any friend of Miss Lydia is a friend of mine—but how can we repay you—if you insist, will you do me the honor of allowing me to buy you a cup of coffee as well . . .*

Wickham! Buying two books and coffee! He must have been very lucky at cards.

Esther Lovett has become very friendly with me since that afternoon. She sought me out the following morning after my bathe, and insisted on drinking chocolate with me. The day after that, she came to the Steine with her mother in the evening, and took tea with us at the Castle Inn, and today she suggested we go shopping. Each time, Wickham contrives to be near. I suspect him of spending yet more of his ill-gained money on this affair, and bribing both Sally and Mrs. Lovett's maid for information as to Esther's movements. He never lingers—a cheery good morning, a brief exchange of pleasantries, and he is on his way again, but it is enough each time to send Miss Lovett into paroxysms of blushing. I do not like it one little bit—either for Esther's sake or for mine, for if he ruins her, they will surely remember that it was I who introduced them! All my chances will be dashed.

I have not seen the Comte and Comtesse again, because Alaric's cold has retained him at Tara all week, and his sister has stayed behind to nurse him. I have written a note, expressing my hope that he should recover soon, and received a reply today. Theo writes that his health is improving, she is ready for my second fitting, and the trap will come for me tomorrow.

I am not going to think about Wickham now.

FRIDAY, 10TH JULY

Theo sent Mrs. Lovett's coachman with the trap. He set
me down by the stables again, and I ran through the
tunnel of trees to the house. As usual, it was quiet. I
skipped through the hall, then remembered Mrs. Lovett's disapproval the last time she found me here, and walked more deco-
rously through the drawing room in case she should see me.

Alaric was sitting on the terrace in an easy chair, a blanket
tucked about his legs and a book upon his lap. He looked up as
I approached and beamed.

"Miss Bennet! I did not know that you were coming today."

"I am come for a fitting. I was on my way down to the
summerhouse. But you are still not well?"

"Oh, it was only a little cold, but Theo fusses and I indulge her by doing exactly as she orders. Have you seen your dress?"

"Not yet, but I'm sure it will be beautiful."

"Oh, it will! Theo is very clever."

I smiled and sat down beside him. "You are very proud of your sister."

"She is everything in the world to me, and we have promised always to take care of each other. But I believe Esther is down there now—will you run in and interrupt them, or will you sit with me? I hope that you will choose the latter, because it has been vastly lonely up here these last few days, and I have missed having company."

He blushed a little as he said that. I pretended not to notice, but my heart beat a little faster.

"Shall I ask for tea?" He did not wait for my answer, but rose from his easy chair and stepped back into the house. I heard him calling out orders in French.

It is a lovely language. I told myself I should like to learn it one day, but that was before . . . My gaze fell upon his book, lying on the floor. It was written in a strange script I could not read.

"What language is *that*?" I asked, when Alaric came back.

"This?" He picked up the book and handed it to me. "It is Sanskrit."

"Oh, of course it is, to be sure!" I blurted.

Alaric looked at me curiously—what could I say?

"I have studied it a little." Even as I spoke, my conscience screamed at me to stop. "Though I have forgotten most of it," I added hurriedly. "Tell me about India! Are you dreadfully home-sick for it?"

It is exactly the right thing to do with Alaric—ask him a question when you want to divert attention. He launched imme-diately into an enthusiastic description.

"India is all color," he said, sweeping his arms about wildly to indicate the flowers in the Tara garden, in case I should not understand what color was. "It is like all of Theo's silks and cottons, and blazing skies such as you never see in England, not even on the hottest day in summer. I miss those colors more than I can say, almost more than the people we left behind. You know, we are so isolated here, but it was not the case in India. We had so many friends there . . . And I miss—oh, the *vastness* of it. The sense you get with every dawn that the whole world is waking up with you, the epic myths about heroes and gods, the hills that turn blue in the afternoon and seem to go on forever. You could spend a lifetime in India and only scratch the surface of its secrets."

He stopped, and gazed at me earnestly. "Do you understand?"

"It sounds wonderful," I said politely.

"Tell her about the other things as well." Theo had arrived without either of us noticing, and her clear voice made me jump. I looked up from my seat, shading my eyes to see her, but the sun was too bright and I could not read her face. "Tell her about the poverty, and the disease, the greed and ambition and injustice."

"If *I* lived in India," Alaric interrupted, "I would live high in the hills, and build a tea plantation."

"Goodness!" I said. "Tea!"

"And I have very clear ideas of how I would run it. *My* plantation would be a fair place, with decent wages for all the workers, and proper housing for their families. I have drawn plans for it. I can show you, if you are interested."

"If you lived in India, you would die," Theo snapped. "Just like *Maman* did. Miss Bennet, I am ready for you in the workroom."

∽✺∽

I cannot lie, I'm afraid. I found my gown disappointingly plain (though no doubt Mrs. Conway would approve). Theo had made a calico of the basic pattern: the bodice is fitted and structured, the sleeves little more than wide straps that lie flat upon the shoulders, the skirt stiff and straight. She busied herself about me for half an hour, frowning in concentration, her small white teeth clamped onto her lower lip making her look vaguely like Napoleon on the prowl, and she seemed so cross that I did not dare say a word until she spoke.

"Of course it will fall better in muslin," she said, as I slipped back into my own clothes. "And I have not yet decided on adornments."

"But there will be adornments?"

"Yes," she said bad-temperedly. "There will be adornments. Come back on Monday for the next fitting."

Alaric and Miss Lovett were talking together on the terrace as I left, the book of Sanskrit open between them. Alaric called out to me in a language I did not understand—was it French, or Sanskrit, or yet another language I do not know? I did not stop to speak to them, but asked instead to be taken straight back to town, and as soon as I arrived I ran straight to the library.

I have to learn Sanskrit by Monday.

SUNDAY, 12TH JULY

*I*t is impossible to keep up with Alaric. One day it is Rousseau and Shakespeare, the next it is this impossible language called Sanskrit. How am I supposed to make sense of it? It looks like nothing I have ever seen in my life before. What on earth possessed people to write their language in shapes and squiggles that nobody can understand, when we have a perfectly good alphabet they can use? The librarian nearly fainted when I told him I needed a book for learning Sanskrit, and yet he was very proud of himself for being able to produce it. "It is from my own private collection," he told me. "Generally speaking, there is not much call for this sort of work in Brighton." He tried to teach me a little of the alphabet, but ten minutes was enough to give me a blinding headache. I brought it home with me to read in bed, together with a travelogue written by a gentleman who traveled all over India, which the librarian described as "very accessible and amusing."

If I show sufficient knowledge of India, perhaps Alaric will not notice my total lack of understanding of its language—or rather, of one of its languages. The librarian tells me they have hundreds! Hundreds! But my mind is so overwrought that nothing will stick. All I have retained so far from my reading is that in India there are fruit like bananas and coconuts and mangoes and guavas, and elephants that go into temples, which are considerably more lively than churches, and birds that repeat words that are spoken to them. Is this enough? Do I have to know the history of *everything*? And oh God, WHY did I say I once studied Sanskrit? Lizzy would never have said such a thing. And why did I never learn French?

And I have not read one *line* of *Macbeth* . . .

I have not been outside for days, and Harriet is worried.

"Come to the beach with me this morning," she coaxed.

"I have to study!"

She enlisted Wickham's help, but I refused to see him. "I saw your friends yesterday," he said through the door of my bedroom. "The Comte de Fombelle was on the Steine with his sister and cousin. Miss Lovett introduced us, and he specifically asked after you."

"I don't care! I can't see them! Go away! I'm busy!"

"Lydia, don't you think you are overdoing this?"

"GO AWAY!"

Oh God, the boredom! But I must go to Tara tomorrow for the next fitting. I can do this. I *can* do this. I CAN DO THIS!

MONDAY, 13TH JULY

Again it was Mrs. Lovett's coachman who, after running some errands in town, fetched me from Brighton in the trap. I felt ill as we drove up, my head bursting with all I had recently read, my lips desperately trying to form the few words of Sanskrit the librarian had endeavored to teach me. I was going to be discovered . . . Alaric would know me for a liar . . . My new life as the friend of a count was over forever . . .

The day was dull and gray, the light dim. The Indian palace on the cliff looked forlorn without bright sunshine, and when I went inside I found that the general mood was no better. Esther

Lovett sat weeping upon the sofa in the drawing room, with her mother on one side and Theo on the other. They appeared to be scolding her, but ceased as soon as I appeared. Even Patch seemed dejected—he lay with his head on Esther's lap, and greeted me with a halfhearted yip instead of his usual bark.

This was Wickham's doing, I was sure of it.

"Miss Bennet!"

"I am come for my fitting," I said. "You sent the trap?"

"To be sure." Theo frowned. Esther Lovett continued to weep. "Miss Bennet . . . Oh, Esther, dear, do stop . . . Miss Bennet, you catch us at a bad time . . ."

"Esther, come for a walk." Mrs. Lovett rose, and pulled her daughter to her feet. "Théodorine, dear . . ."

Theo looked at me—hesitated—looked at Miss Lovett, and appeared to reach a decision. "I will accompany you," she said. "Miss Bennet, please excuse me. I shan't be long—half an hour at the most—if you go to my workroom, you will find the latest *Belle Assemblée*, with some very pretty new plates. Perhaps you would like . . ."

"Of course." I was astonished at her rudeness, but what else could I say? And then they were gone.

I wandered down to the summerhouse, found the periodical, and was just settled at the worktable to read it (oh, the bliss of fashion plates after two days of Sanskrit!), when the door opened and Alaric peered in.

"Is the coast clear?" he asked. "Is it safe?"

"They have left for a walk." I tried to smile, but my heart leaped with alarm at the sight of him. "But what was the meaning of all the commotion?"

"It is poor Esther," he said. "They will not tell me what exactly is going on. I know only that my aunt's maid has been dismissed, and that Esther will not stop crying, and that my aunt is angry. I cannot think why. Esther is the very best sort of person, and I'm quite sure she has done nothing wrong, but now my aunt will not allow her to leave the house. And so . . ." He shrugged, and gestured vaguely in the direction of the path leading from the house to the cliffs, where Mrs. Lovett, her daughter, and niece were presumably walking.

"But how cold it is in here!" he said. "This terrible English weather! I have a small fire in my room upstairs—if you do not think it improper, shall we sit by it? I can show you my drawings, if you like—of the tea plantation, you know."

I nodded and followed, swallowing my apprehension. This was the moment, I was sure of it, when all my lies were to be uncovered and I would lose everything I had worked so hard to gain.

In the attic Alaric went straight to his drawing table, pulled out some papers, and began to talk, eyes shining as he explained. I tried to concentrate, but it was hard to understand. Outside, the sun had broken through the clouds, and I thought longingly of the sea.

"So you see, with the right drainage, levels of hygiene and

sanitation would be vastly improved," Alaric finished, a little out of breath. "What do you think?"

What did I think? Of hygiene and sanitation? Of his drawings? I had no idea! I had to change the subject.

"Are you looking forward to the ball?" I blurted.

"The ball?" He looked startled. "Lord, I hadn't thought! I suppose . . . why, no!"

"No!" This was inconceivable. "But it is a ball!"

"The truth is, Miss Bennet, I am not a very good dancer."

"That is because you are so clever," I told him. "You most likely think too hard about it. Dancing is something you must feel in your feet—indeed, in your whole body. Come, I will show you."

I seized his hand, and tried to pull him away from the table. He did not follow, but stared at me astonished.

"Oh," I faltered, dropping his hand. "You think me forward. I am so sorry. My sister Kitty and I—we practice all the time. I did not mean—that is, I had no thought of—I mean, I just thought, if you like—I could teach you to dance."

He was blushing, the deepest I have ever seen any man. I felt myself redden as well.

"I am sorry," I repeated. "It was silly, and I did not think, and I should not have . . ."

"No!" he said, with such violence I started from surprise. "No," he said more gently. "It was kind. And I should like to learn to dance."

He stepped toward me, and took both my hands in his. "I should like it very much."

It is not easy to dance without music with someone who does not know what he is doing. We started on a simple country dance, and at first Alaric fumbled. He took my hand at the wrong moment, stepped in when he should have waited, turned about when he should have stepped in. After our first clumsy attempts, I began to hum to encourage him. He picked up the tune and hummed it back. Slowly, at first, and then faster, I led him up the room. Back down we came, promenading separately, weaving our way through imaginary dancers, and I was smiling so hard it hurt.

This I *am* good at, I thought. With this I don't need to pretend. And look at me! Dancing with a count!

We ended where we had started, facing each other at the far window by his drawing table, our eyes locked and our breath quick and our right palms joined, and I thought, This is it! *This* is my future!

"You see." I smiled. "You can dance."

"That is because you are a good teacher," he whispered.

I dropped my hand and threw myself onto the sofa to hide my pleasure.

"Lord!" I exclaimed. "No one has ever called me *that* before. How my sister Mary would laugh!"

Alaric sat carefully in an armchair opposite me. "Why so?" he asked.

"Oh!" I scoffed, without thinking. "Mary has little time for dancing, or any form of merriment. She is the most tiresome person in the world, forever learning and always at her books— oh God!"

I clapped my hand over my mouth and stared at him, horrified. Then, unable to hold his gaze, I lowered my eyes to the floor.

"Miss Bennet? Miss Bennet, what is wrong?"

I sensed him move, and then he was sitting beside me. I buried my face in my hands.

"I wanted to meet you!" I wailed. "All of you. You are so— different from anyone I ever saw or met before. But you are all so clever, and I am so stupid—no, don't say I am not! I know I am—everyone says so. And then Saint Augustine . . . Mr. Collins . . . It was too good to be true! I promise I *have* been reading since I met you—incessantly, and quite the dullest books you can imagine. But until we met, I couldn't care less about learning or reading. I don't even know where India is—I have been trying to read about it, but I felt too stupid to ask the librarian to show me on his globe!"

I cried then—actual proper tears. Alaric said nothing.

It is over, I thought. He is disgusted with me. He will never speak to me again.

Then—a tug on my hand. Alaric stood up, pulling me with him. And now it was he who led me across the room, around the furniture I had moved for our dance, until we were standing before his globe, which he slowly spun with his free hand.

"There!" He placed my hand on a sort of misshaped

diamond, wide across and pointy at the bottom, surrounded by sea.

"There," he repeated. "There is India."

Shaking a little, I traced it with my finger. "And where are we?" I asked.

He spun the globe back. "Here," he said. "These are the British Isles."

"But they are so small!" I stared, astonished. I walked around the table to look at India, at least twenty times the size of Great Britain. "Why, it is halfway across the world."

"It is six months away by boat."

He showed me the path a boat must take to sail from Southampton to Madras, where his stepfather still lives.

"Six months!" I breathed. "I had no idea anything could be so far away!"

He smiled and led me back toward the fire. I trembled again as I waited for him to speak.

"You are actually a hopeless liar, you know," he said, his eyes sparkling. "You have been twice inside this room and not once looked to see what volumes are upon the shelves. A true reader would not have done that—her eyes would be continually turning to the books. And since that first time I drove you to Tara, you have never once referred to another book—not even after I lent you *Macbeth*. It won't do, Lydia. Lying is not something that can be done by halves. If you must lie, you have to lie to the end."

I was struggling to understand.

"So . . . you don't mind?" I stammered.

"Mind? I couldn't care less! Miss Bennet . . ." He blushed again. I held my breath, and stared again at the floor. "Miss Bennet, you must know how much I admire you."

"Admire me?" I gasped. "Even though I don't read?"

"Tremendously!" He was becoming himself again—talking, talking, talking! "Your energy, your laughter! The way you look at the world, like it is a grand adventure, just waiting for you . . . Miss Bennet, I . . ."

He strode forward and took me in his arms.

Here is what happens when a boy kisses you.

There is a moment when time seems to stop, and the air goes very still between you, and it feels like you are being pulled together by an invisible force. He closes his eyes, but you keep yours open because you don't want to miss a second of what is happening, and though he looks funny with his eyes shut—so concentrated, like my Gardiner cousins trying to remember their lessons—you don't laugh, because he also looks so serious and a little like he is in pain, and the distance between you closes, and your noses bump, but then his lips are on yours, and they are a bit damp and his breath is heavy but it is—oh, it is the sweetest thing in the world.

"Lydia," he whispered, as we broke away. "May I call you Lydia?"

"You may," I replied.

"Lydia, please don't ever change."

He kissed me again. This time our noses did not collide, and his arms were just closing about me when there was a familiar clatter on the stairs outside, Theo calling out, "We are back! Alaric? Miss Bennet?" We sprang apart, Alaric tripping over a low table in his haste.

Theo pulled and prodded and jabbed me with needles this afternoon, but I could not focus on my fitting. She is pleased with the way the dress is coming along, but I cannot remember a single detail of it. Alaric kissed me! He doesn't care about the books! He doesn't want me to change! Ha! What would Lizzy say to that! *He* doesn't think me *idle* and *vain and ignorant*! And as for Wickham and all his threats to unmask me—what are they now? The Comte Alaric de Fombelle-Aix-Jouvet *admires me tremendously*! He kissed me! Why, we are as good as engaged. Just wait until I tell my sisters!

BRIGHTON
MONDAY, 13TH JULY

DEAR KITTY,

REMEMBER THAT I WROTE TO YOU ABOUT HOW A FRENCH
COMTESSE WAS MAKING ME A DRESS? WELL, I AM BECOME
EXCEEDINGLY CLOSE TO HER BROTHER! WE ARE MONSTROUS
FOND OF EACH OTHER. IMAGINE ME A COUNTESS, KITTY! WOULD
NOT THAT BE A HOOT! WE WILL LIVE HERE IN BRIGHTON IN HIS
FAMILY HOME, THOUGH I SHOULD ALSO LIKE A HOUSE IN
LONDON-THAT WOULD BE ONLY RIGHT, I THINK, BECAUSE ALARIC
WILL WANT TO BE NEAR ST. JAMES'S. AND WE WILL FIND YOU
A NICE LORD CLOSE BY, SO THAT WE CAN BE LADIES TOGETHER!

MORE SOON!
LYDIA (YOUR ALMOST ROYAL SISTER)

TUESDAY, 14TH JULY

I woke up laughing.

The sun is back, and the sky is bright, bright blue, and I think that every bird in the world has come to Brighton to sing. Alaric sent word after breakfast that they would pick me up at three o'clock to drive to the Rookery at Preston Manor for tea—"for poor Esther must have an outing," he wrote, "and Preston being some distance from town, my aunt has agreed to it."

Alaric drove, with Theo beside him. I did not know how to greet him. A lady may not very well kiss a gentleman in public! I contented myself with a demure curtsy in response to his bow, but then as he helped me into the trap after Esther, I allowed my hand to linger in his, and he briefly squeezed it.

That was all but it was *thrilling*. And then, over tea, he recited Shakespeare, but it didn't feel dusty or boring, because he loves Shakespeare like I love Napoleon and dancing and running about. He *lives* it, and right there at the table, he actually beat his chest to demonstrate the violence of Romeo's passion.

"But soft! What light through yonder window breaks? It is the east, and Juliet is the sun.

Arise, fair sun, and kill the envious moon."

"For heaven's sake, Alaric, people are watching," Theo said, and I had to turn away to hide my smile, because I knew those verses were just for me.

If *I* wrote *Romeo and Juliet*, I wouldn't kill them at all. I would have them run away to a beautiful island where they would be free to dance and swim about all day, and eat peaches in the sun, and be incandescently happy in spite of their horrible families. I told Alaric as much and he thought it the funniest thing he had ever heard, and said what a shame Shakespeare was dead, or we could go together to London and demand he incorporate my suggestions immediately.

London!

Oh, why does he not propose? This secrecy is delicious, but I cannot wait for the world to know . . .

When I am Lydia, the Comtesse de Fombelle, I will live at Tara in a room painted green and white and gold and eat sweet rolls every day for breakfast. And when the war is over, I will pack a trunk full of traveling clothes and Alaric and I will roam all over Europe—France and Greece and Spain. Perhaps we can find his family castle, the one that was stolen in the Revolution, and make them give it back. And we will go swimming in the Mediterranean Sea, and I will wear silk dresses to the beach, and play cricket with a dozen lacy parasols. I will ride about on a dear little donkey, and Napoleon shall have fish every day for supper.

WEDNESDAY, 15TH JULY

Sally knocked at my door this morning as I was dressing.

"Gentleman for you in the parlor, Miss," she told me, and my heart leaped. At last! I thought. Alaric has come to propose!

Harriet was not yet ready. I ran down, happy in the knowledge that we would be alone, yet despairing of the fact that we were in Market Street—I did not want a proposal here! I wanted it at Tara, or on a windswept beach. But oh, it did not matter! Soon, everyone would know . . . Alaric would write to Father . . . I would walk into the next ball with a sparkling ring on my finger . . .

I stopped at the foot of the stairs to assume my most modest expression, pushed open the door—Wickham, not Alaric, stood upon the hearth.

"A walk, young Lydia," he said.

My disappointment was so great, I could not protest. I took my shawl and bonnet from the chair where I had left them yesterday, and followed him out of the house.

"I need you to deliver a message to Miss Lovett," Wickham said as we set out toward the sea. "Now that the maid is gone."

I frowned, remembering. Esther, crying on the sofa . . . Goodness, I hadn't given her a moment's thought! "The maid was dismissed," I said. "Was that because of you? What has happened?"

"Nothing has happened," he said impatiently. "Nor is it going to, if I can't see her."

"But what of the maid . . ."

"The maid was giving me information, as you know. There was a note . . ."

"A *note*?"

"Oh, do not worry, my name was not on it. But it was found, and the whole situation blown out of all proportion . . ."

"Out of all proportion! What did you write, in this *note*?"

"I professed my ardent love for her, and asked her to meet me."

"Love her! Meet you! Since when are you and Miss Lovett on such intimate terms? I admit you excelled yourself on your first meeting, but since then you have never said more than *good morning* to her, or exchanged pleasantries about the weather!"

"Our paths have crossed a great deal."

"When? How was I not aware of this?"

"You were *studying.*"

Dimly, I recollected Wickham outside my bedroom door, exhorting me to stop reading—*I saw the Comte de Fombelle last night . . . Miss Lovett introduced us . . .*

"Goodness! You *have* been busy," I said grimly. "And now you are found out again. You are making quite a habit of this. I wonder you have been so clumsy"

He ignored me.

"I need you to give a message to Miss Lovett for me."

"A message! But why would I do that?"

"Lydia, we have spoken of this."

I felt very powerful, suddenly, when he said that. It was a new feeling, and I liked it.

"You are referring, I think, to your attempt to blackmail me?" I murmured. "Circumstances have altered. I find I am no longer at all afraid of you."

"Don't tell me he has proposed!"

"He has *not* proposed," I admitted. "Yet! But he knows all about the books and the learning, and he couldn't care less because *he admires me tremendously.*"

Wickham walked beside me for a while in thoughtful silence.

"I'll admit, this changes things," he said.

"It does indeed."

"And what does Mademoiselle his sister think, of this tremendous admiration?"

"His sister?"

"Does she not know? Well, well, I can't say I blame the boy. She is hardly likely to approve the match, and from what I have seen of her, if she were *my* sister, I, too, would be afraid of her reaction."

"You are wrong," I said hotly, but even as I spoke doubt began to creep in. I recalled the way Alaric sprang away from me in his attic, when he heard her coming upstairs . . . Did he spring a little too fast? His discretion yesterday at the Rookery . . . I thought he was protecting my honor, but could it have been a mask for fear? And if so . . . what of my proposal?

"The countess is excessively fond of me," I stammered.

"I'm quite sure she loves you like a sister," Wickham said. "My question was, how much does she know? I feel someone ought to tell her the truth."

My mind began to race as I understood what he was saying.

If I help Wickham . . . If Theo or Mrs. Lovett should find out . . . They will be furious . . . They will hate me!

"I have had word from Miss Lovett," Wickham continued. "She succeeded in smuggling a letter to me by post, in which she entreats me not to communicate with her again. Though she adores me—"

"Adores you!"

"Yes." Oh, how smug he looked! "But let me finish. Though she adores me, as I say, she must give me up, for the sake of her mamma, who would not approve, et cetera, et cetera—all the usual reasons. The message I want you to give her . . ."

"I won't do it!"

"Hear me out, Lydia. It is innocent enough. I merely ask that you beg her, on my behalf, for the honor of one dance at tomorrow's dress ball."

"One dance?" I was astonished. "That is all?"

"That is all. Tell her I have received her letter and will obey her wishes, but that the precious memory of just one dance with her will act as a light in my darkness for the lonely decades to come."

"That is *revolting*!" I snorted. "No woman could fall for that."

"It isn't revolting, it's romantic."

"It's revolting. And they probably won't let her go to the ball, you know. There was a terrible fuss about the maid."

"She *will* be at the ball," he said, "for two reasons. The dress ball is one of the most important events of the Brighton season, something Mrs. Lovett cares deeply about. And Miss Lovett's cousin, the Comtesse de Fombelle, has made her a dress especially for the occasion, and is anxious for her to show it off. Miss Lovett herself has professed complete ignorance as to the identity of the person who penned the letter, and after much weeping has convinced her mamma that she harbors no illicit feelings toward anyone."

"You are very well informed."

"It was a very long letter."

The tide was turning, and the waves had grown a little rougher. Perfect for diving under, I thought. Perfect for escaping.

"Just one dance?" I said. "You promise there will be nothing more?"

"Just one dance, and then I shan't ask you ever to intervene with Miss Lovett again. Come, Lydia—what harm can it do?"

"Very well," I said. "One dance."

We walked back separately, he cutting through town, I walking along the front. The days are so long now! The sun showed no sign of setting, but I was so tired.

I have not forgotten Georgiana Darcy, or Wickham's broken promise to me. I do not trust him. But what can I do? Until Alaric proposes, I cannot risk Theo finding out about us.

❧

There was a letter waiting for me at home from Jane. No note, but a charcoal drawing of Napoleon napping on my pillow. "Someone who can't wait to see you again," Jane has written on the back. It is not the *best* drawing of a cat. His head is too large, and his back paws a most peculiar shape. But it is most definitely him, and I know that it is my pillow because I recognize the lace-edged case Kitty gave me at Christmas, with *L.B.* embroidered in the corner.

I kissed the drawing, and then pasted it into my diary. Not because I love it—I do love it, but that is not the reason. It is a reminder of everything I never want to go back to.

Alaric *will* propose to me, I know he will.

And what difference can one dance make?

THURSDAY, 16TH JULY
THE DRESS BALL!

*H*arriet protested that I should prepare for the ball with her, but Theo insisted that I go to Tara. "It is very important to my sister," Alaric explained, when he came to fetch me. "She wishes to supervise every detail of how her gowns are worn."

Harriet is still torn between disapproval of Theo's dress-making ambitions and jealousy of me having a dress made by a countess, but she could not bring herself to argue with a count. We escaped Market Street with promises of good behavior on my part, and good care on his.

"And I have you to myself for half an hour!" he gloated as the trap trotted out of town. He took my hand firmly in his, and my heart soared. We turned onto the cliff road. The mare munched on the hedgerow, as Alaric pressed me in his arms.

"*Now*," I thought. "He will ask me now."

"How. lovely you are!" He sighed. "I will never tire of the sight of you."

I almost asked him, then, if he had told his sister about us. And if not, when he intended to—*whether* he intended to . . .

I must marry him, I thought.

A pheasant took off in the hedge, with a great clacking of wings. The mare spooked and broke into a canter, throwing us backward. I clung to the seat. Alaric almost tumbled out of the trap, but managed to save himself by clinging to the frame.

"Your hat!" I cried, seeing it roll into the ditch.

"I'll come back for it later!" he shouted. "Wretched creature! She might have killed us!"

He looked so funny, thrown this way and that by the errant mare, his hair blowing madly in the wind. I burst out laughing, and decided not to say a thing.

The weather was fine, and the countryside was lovely, and I had a new dress, and I was going to a ball. What else should I be thinking of, on a day like this?

There would be time enough later for everything else.

∞

I gave Esther Lovett Wickham's message as soon as I saw. her. She was alone at the piano, Alaric unhitching the mare, Theo in her workroom, Mrs. Lovett in the garden tending roses. I told

Esther word for word what he instructed me to say, right down to the dance being his one light in a dark, dark future.

She didn't think it was revolting. In fact, she cried a little, and thanked me.

Really, it is rather sweet.

In France, before the Revolution, when Alaric and Theo's family still owned their castle, the housekeeper Marie used to prepare their *maman* for appearances at court where, she says, the fashions set by Marie Antoinette were more elaborate than anything ever seen in England. She worked on Esther and me for hours—filed and buffed our nails, plucked and shaped our eyebrows, pulled our hair this way and that, combed it, parted it, curled and primped it. She tied mine high on my head in a tumble of Grecian curls with a ribbon of amber velvet and two silver gilt combs, and smoothed Esther's into a heavy chignon held in a net of pearls. She rubbed our faces with lotion, added color to Esther's pale cheeks and toned down the excessive ruddiness of mine, smeared a hint of pink on our lips, and clipped my jade earrings to my ears and pearls to Esther's.

"I never wear jewelry," Esther protested.

"You do today, *mademoiselle*."

Finally—*finally!*—she declared us ready for the Comtesse.

My dress is white, but it is not as plain as the calico suggested. Theo has added an overlay of gold gauze, rising in puffs above the neck and shoulders, fitted to the bodice and floating to the floor, and she has trimmed the neckline with the same amber velvet ribbon Marie used in my hair. The style makes me look even taller than I am, and the white and gold bring out the color of my skin, darkened to deep tan despite my efforts to protect it from the sun.

"Exactly the effect I was hoping for," Theo murmured as she made some final adjustments to my sleeves. "Simple, elegant, and athletic. You will be much admired, Miss Bennet. Now, I must see to Esther."

I gazed at my reflection in the summerhouse looking glass. The girl in the mirror stared back, and you could tell, even without knowing her, that here was a girl who loved to dance and laugh and run and swim, but the gold lent a softness to my appearance as well, giving me a fragile look I was not used to. I was pleased—until I looked across at Esther.

Until today, I have only ever seen Esther wear pale, dull colors. This evening, Theo dressed her in one of her rich Indian silks, a deep blue green with a high waist and low neck, embroidered with pearls, trimmed with pink velvet, and in her hair, not one, not two, but *three* delicate ostrich feathers of the same color, held by a silver circlet.

Gone was the timid vole. In her place, radiant and glowing, was a tiny, dainty beauty. Theo had said she would make me look like a princess, but next to Esther, I was more like a cart horse.

"Just what I wanted," Theo repeated happily, and I glanced at her suspiciously. "After tonight, everyone will want to be dressed by me."

Had she done it on purpose?

Theo dressed quickly, almost carelessly, in a light-green dress of utmost simplicity that made her hair blaze and gave her an almost fairylike appearance. Marie brought mantles, especially made by Theo to complement the dresses, and together we all walked up the path to where Alaric and Mrs. Lovett waited on the terrace.

"Well, Théodorine!" Mrs. Lovett said. "I must say you have excelled yourself. She looks beautiful."

Miss Lovett blushed at her mother's rudeness. "You mean *we* look beautiful, Mamma. I am sure I never saw anyone look as lovely as Miss Bennet."

She is far too good for Wickham.

"Quite right, Esther," Alaric said stoutly. "Theo, you are a clever old thing. Esther, Miss Bennet—you are both visions. Esther is like an exquisite china doll. Miss Bennet, like a Greek goddess."

His hand found mine as we walked toward Mrs. Lovett's carriage. A brief squeeze gave me renewed heart. A murmured "Ignore my aunt" and "I prefer goddesses," even more so.

∽e෴ා

Theo wanted to make an entrance, and we arrived after the ball had started. The master of ceremonies introduced us and heads whipped round to stare. It is—oh, it is a very different sensation, to arrive well dressed at a smart ball, rather than in your sister's hand-me-downs. In a room full of people, I no longer compared myself to tiny Esther. My dress was light and graceful. I sensed the approval in people's gazes as I moved about the room. Harriet rushed up, in lilac with pompadour tassels, admired me, congratulated Theo. The Colonel came behind her, all compliments as well.

I never want to wear any other sort of clothes again—I may even wear this dress for my wedding . . . but I am getting ahead of myself, as usual.

Into the ball we went. How splendid everything was! Though I have been in the Ship's ballroom several times since arriving here, tonight was different—infinitely more candles, an orchestra twice the usual size, great garlands of lilies and roses, and the dresses! But none more splendid than mine (and Esther's). Oh, if Caroline Bingley had seen me tonight!

The orchestra was striking up.

"It is the dance I showed you," I whispered to Alaric, who grinned, and bowed, and held out his arm. Theo frowned but he ignored her. *He ignored her!*

"You have been practicing," I murmured as we promenaded together, with barely a trip or fumble on his part.

"Endlessly!" He smiled.

For a moment, as we came to a stop, our right hands joined, I felt it again—the certainty I had when we danced without music in his attic room, that this was my future. But then . . .

"I must dance with Esther," he said. "If I could, I would dance with only you all night, but Theo is very particular, you know, about etiquette, and says I must not dance with anyone more than once."

"Is she?" I could not think of anyone less particular about etiquette than the Comtesse de Fombelle.

"I shall dance abysmally, of course. I think I am only able to dance well with you . . ."

Off he went, to ask Esther to dance. A gentleman I did not know stepped up and invited me. It was a reel, and we danced well together, but my heart was not in it.

Oh, why did he not stand up to his sister?

There was a flurry of scarlet by the door, and the officers of the Derbyshire strode in, with Wickham among them. I peeped over my partner's shoulder at Esther—had she seen him? Of course she had. She was ghostly pale despite the exertion of the reel, though making a great show of enjoying Alaric's appalling dancing. I looked at her mother. Mrs. Lovett watched her daughter with a pleased smile, unaware that danger had entered the room. Wickham was right—she knew nothing of the identity of her daughter's secret admirer!

Three more dances before Wickham made his move, during which everyone changed partners. I danced with Denny, and Carter, then someone else. Wickham danced with Harriet, and the wives of two other officers. Alaric, his duty done, stood aside, and Esther danced with three gentlemen I had never seen before, until finally Mrs. Lovett and Theo turned away, distracted by the greeting of an acquaintance.

The cotillion began. Wickham was before Esther—he was bowing—she was still pale, but smiling—she was on his arm . . . For a moment, watching them together, I felt a pang of envy. How well they danced! I remembered my waltz with Wickham on my birthday—our merry reels at Longbourn . . . Her hand on his as they moved through the dance, her dress brushing his coat as they passed each other, her eyes on his as she faced him in the square—Esther Lovett did not dance, she floated, and it was perfectly obvious that she was incandescent with love. Mrs. Lovett saw it at once, and so did the Comtesse de Fombelle . . .

Suddenly, Alaric was before me, holding out his hand. My heart leaped. I forgot all about Wickham and Esther.

"*Two* dances?" I murmured.

Did I imagine a tiny glance toward his sister? Together, we joined the dance. Theo was watching us, her face all dark emotion.

"Your sister is displeased," I warned Alaric. And then—oh, I thought I was going to burst!

Alaric stepped right up to me—much closer than the dance allowed—and whispered, "Let her be displeased! I only dance well with you."

Theo and Mrs. Lovett were talking together, their eyes darting from Esther and Wickham to me and Alaric, but why should I care? I was Lydia Bennet from Meryton, dancing with a count! Alaric trod all over my feet, but happiness gave me wings. No matter that he did not know the steps—I danced like an angel for both of us.

"Will you meet me tomorrow?" he asked as the dance finished.

"Of course!"

"I will pick you up at the library at two o'clock. We will go for a drive. Oh, Lydia!"

Across the spinning crowds, my eyes met Theo's. I could not resist a smile of triumph.

Theo and Mrs. Lovett were upon us with the closing bars of the cotillion, marching Esther away from the ball, a grinning Alaric in their wake.

I danced late into the night—I could have danced until dawn. The sky was already lightening when I finally left the Ship with Harriet and Colonel Forster. If they had let me, I would have run to the beach and danced right there on the shore as dawn broke around me.

Let her be displeased! he said. *I only dance well with you!*

My very own count! When I am Lydia, Comtesse de Fombelle . . . But I am not going to think about that now.

FRIDAY, 17TH JULY

*I*t has failed spectacularly for Wickham, but I SHOULD THANK HIM. I ought to run right up to the barracks and KISS HIM for what he has done for me, because without him . . .

Too fast, too fast! I must start from the beginning.

I was woken from delicious dreams this morning by Harriet, yelling from the parlor that I had a visitor. "I am still in bed!" I shouted, and then a little voice called up saying that it didn't matter, and "Please, Lydia, may I come up?" and Esther was in my room red-eyed and mousy again, and I was sitting up in bed, pulling the covers about me to make room for her.

"I am come to say good-bye," she said.

"Good-bye! Why, Miss Lovett, what do you mean? You are not well. I'm sorry, there is nowhere to sit . . ."

She perched her tiny frame on the end of my bed.

"I shan't stay long—Mamma thinks I am at the library, returning books. Dear Miss Bennet, I wanted only to thank you for your kindness."

"My kindness?"

"In what you did—convincing me so eloquently of Mr. Wickham's feelings. Oh, Miss Bennet! I have to tell you . . . last night, as we danced, he begged me to marry him!"

"Did he?" I was astonished. Even for Wickham, this seemed wildly optimistic. "What did you say?"

"I could not . . . that is, I did not want to . . . Oh, Miss Bennet, I did not want to hurt him! I said that I would think about it. But later, after the ball—Mamma and Theo forced the truth out of me, and determined immediately that I should leave Brighton. Mamma says that she knows his type very well, and that she will never allow it, and . . . I am not fearless like you, Miss Bennet. I could not swim in the open sea or travel about without my family . . . so I certainly could not defy Mamma, even though I am sure he cannot be as bad as she says he is. After all, he is a friend of yours!"

I smiled weakly.

"And so now I must ask you—oh, Miss Bennet, it is a sad favor—I can see that I did wrong to encourage him last night. Will you tell him . . . will you tell him for me that it is hopeless?

But that . . . oh, that I enjoyed our dance *very much*! He is a good dancer, is he not?"

"He is," I admitted.

"And you will tell him?"

"I will."

She clasped my hands in hers, and raised them to her lips. I do not know when I was ever more uncomfortable.

"When do you leave?" I asked, to change the subject.

"Tomorrow. We go to London first, to Grosvenor Square, and from there to Mapperton Lacey—to my estate in Shropshire."

And then she said, "At least I shan't be alone. My cousins have agreed to come with us."

Alaric, leaving too! I was furious. Furious! I could not hold still, my rage was so great. It was a terrible day—wet and blowy and cold. After Esther left I dressed in the first clothes I could find, threw on my traveling cloak, and stormed down to the beach. The waves today were as tall as houses. There wasn't a single bathing machine out, and the fishermen's boats were pulled high up on the shore. I leaned over the edge of the cliff and breathed in the salt air. At the far end, where the beach is narrowest, spray blew up from the water onto my face. If I had been alone, I would have torn off my clothes and thrown myself in.

It was Theo's doing, of course. The way she looked at us at the ball! Whispering with her aunt! *Esther must be removed from that soldier,* I imagined her saying, and, *Heavens! Alaric and Miss*

Bennet! God forbid her common blood should mix with my noble brother's.

Oh, how could this be happening to me?

I went home and changed my dress. I ate some lunch. I tried to read a book, and not to look at the clock.

Harriet said, "If you're waiting for Wickham, he isn't coming. There was a skirmish farther down the coast, some local disturbance. The Colonel has sent a few men to calm it. You shouldn't pine for him, Lydia. The Colonel has quite reached the end of his patience with his gambling, and says he has positively mountains of debts."

"You think I'm pining for *Wickham*?"

"Who else? Goodness! Not that count! As if he would be interested in *you*!"

∾⦵∿

One o'clock. Would he come? Half past. The wait was unbearable! At a quarter to two, as Harriet lay dozing on the sofa, I put on my bonnet and my green cape and slipped out to run to the library.

He was early, sitting holding the reins of the trap, lost in thought. He didn't see me until I was right before him, and when he did see me he didn't speak, but held out a hand to help me up.

"Is it true?" I cried.

"You heard, then. Esther said she had been to see you."

Thunder rumbled in the distance.

"Even the weather is against us," Alaric groaned.

"It will clear," I said. "Look, the storm is far out at sea."

Above us, huge clouds hurried across the gray sky. Alaric stared up at them doubtfully.

"Let's just drive," I said. "Or else we shall have to say good-bye here, and I don't think I could bear that."

He nodded, and we set out at a fast trot, the mare tossing her head at the wind, Alaric for once completely absorbed by the driving. We followed the coast road beyond Hove, stopping eventually at a wide, empty beach. The tide was low. Alaric tied the mare, and together we walked across the shingle and over the packed, damp sand toward the wild sea. At the water's edge, he pulled me into his arms and, as the wind howled about us, squeezed me until I could not breathe.

This cannot be the last time I see him, I thought. I won't let it be.

"Must you go?" I asked.

"I don't know how I can't. They are all in an uproar, though nobody will explain why. They only say that we must leave at once, and that it is to do with poor Esther."

"But if you explained . . ."

"Lydia, there is something I must tell you . . ."

His sister did not approve of us . . . He dared not anger her . . .

"Oh, do not tell me!" I cried. "I do not want to know!"

He kissed me then—out there on the beach, in the open,

with gulls calling their mournful cries above and the waves crashing about us. A wave swept right in to where we were standing, soaking my boots and skirts. It pulled out again, gathering for a fresh attack. I grabbed Alaric's hand, and we ran together to the higher ground, and fell panting on the dry pebbles, lying side by side on our backs.

"I wish we could stay like this forever," he said.

"What, here?"

"Yes, here—just the two of us. Look around, Lydia! There is not another soul for miles. We could run about and shout our heads off and nobody would hear."

"Go on, then," I said.

"What?"

"Run about and shout your head off!"

He hesitated.

"Oh, for heaven's sake!" I jumped to my feet. The first drops of rain were beginning to fall, and I raised my face toward them. "Can you hear me?" I yelled at the clouds. "Don't you dare rain on me!" I began to spin round and round with my arms outstretched, and now Alaric was on his feet as well, spinning beside me.

"I love Lydia Bennet!" he shouted at the sky. "I love her! Can you hear me?"

I stopped turning. Stared at him. He stopped, too, and stared back.

"You love me?" I whispered.

"Yes," he said. "I do. I really do."

And he took me in his arms, and we sheltered together by a bank of pebbles in the lea of the wind, and he kissed me again like the world was about to end, and I kissed him back, and it was different from the other times we had kissed—sad and urgent and a little bit desperate.

In my head, I thought I heard Mamma's voice saying, "When you want something, Lydia, you must fight" and I knew exactly what we had to do.

"Run away with me," I whispered, when we ran out of kisses.

Suddenly, I could see it so clearly. The two of us, wrapped in traveling cloaks, stealing away, galloping through the dead of night in a carriage bound for Scotland, me in a dear hat maybe with a little veil, Alaric dashing in his blue coat . . .

"We'll go to Scotland," I said. "You can get married there in an instant, without licenses or anything."

Alaric was staring again, but now his eyes were wide with shock.

"Lydia! You cannot be serious!"

"Why not? It's what people do, isn't it, when they cannot be together?"

"Only when . . . Lydia, the disgrace! Your reputation! You would be ruined . . ."

What could I say, that might convince him?

"We can go to India!" I cried. "Alaric, your tea plantation!" To be sure, I was a little baffled when he first told me about that, but why not? The elephants and the temples and the delicious fruit, all those silks and fabrics and spices . . . Why not go for a few years, and return even richer than when we left like his own stepfather had?

He was laughing now, raised our joined hands to his lips, smothered mine in kisses.

"We shall have to go to Southampton instead of Scotland," I said. "We will leave tonight—at what time do coaches leave for Southampton?"

"I don't think there is a night coach to Southampton . . ."

"Then we will go to London, and leave for Southampton from there tomorrow morning! That will confuse them if they try to follow us! Alaric, say you will do it!"

A sudden clap of thunder, and the heavens opened. Alaric leaped to his feet and pulled me up. We ran for the trap, pulled the cover over, and crept beneath it.

"And this is summer?" Alaric cried. "The weather in this country!"

"So think of India!" I insisted.

Another peal of thunder. The rain fell harder. The cover bowed. Water splashed our clothes, trickled down our necks . . .

Alaric burst out laughing, and pressed his mouth to mine. "Lydia Bennet, you are quite mad, but I do believe I would do anything for you."

The mare was wretched as we drove back into Brighton, Alaric and I a sodden, bedraggled mess, yet we were both glowing like beacons.

"The coach leaves at nine o'clock," I said. "I know, because the Colonel had to take it once. We are all invited to dine with the other officers tonight, but I shall pretend to be ill and stay behind until they are gone. What will you do?"

"I'll think of something."

We giggled like two conspirators. It was happening! It was real!

He set me down at the top of Market Street.

"Until tonight," I said. "The nine o'clock coach!"

"Parting is such sweet sorrow!" he cried (I think it is from *Romeo and Juliet*). "Until tonight, Lydia!"

He drove away, waving, but I did not turn immediately for home. Instead, and despite the rain, I crossed over the road to look at the sea.

How different I am now from the girl who stood on the platform of Janet's bathing machine, afraid to jump in the water! To think that I can now swim on my own . . .

There are sharks in India, huge great things the size of horses, Alaric says, but they will not bother us. He knows all the best places for bathing. The water will be warm and clear, and the beach will be all white sand. Alaric says that sometimes they build fires on the beach to cook fish they buy from the fishermen—like the fish the Longbourn village boys and I tried to cook all those years ago, but actually edible. Alaric says it is the best food you ever tasted, and they eat it with coconuts straight off the trees. *Coconuts!*

How different it will be—how glorious! But I don't think I shall ever stop loving Brighton.

♾ LATER ♾

My small valise is packed. I am taking only absolute essentials. My lightest summer dresses—the green muslin, the spotted white. I am wearing my altered blue, but when the time comes I shall pack that, too, as well as my dress from the ball, which is far too beautiful to leave behind, regardless of who made it. And my new parasol, which will be so useful against the sun when we are at sea, whatever Theo says about it only being good for cricket. Theo! What will *she* think when we are gone? She will miss her brother . . . But it is her own fault. She should not be trying to come between us.

I have packed my bathing shift, and all my stockings and stays and underclothes, and my dancing slippers and new pantaloons, and two nightgowns and a good shawl. There is no room for my bonnets. I must choose one, which I will wear tonight. After much deliberation, I have settled on the little yellow poke with the tiny crown and the very wide brim that best hides my face—it seems the one most appropriate for running away. And I have packed quantities of different ribbons with which to vary it, to make up for not bringing the others.

The little money I have left.

My diary—I could not leave *that* behind!

The picture Jane drew of Napoleon—because who knows if I shall ever see him again? My sisters and my parents will still be here, when I return from India in a few years' time, with my fine

276

noble husband and pots and pots of money to save them all from destitution, but cats do not live as long as humans, especially cats like Napoleon who roam about the countryside getting into fights and annoying farmers by making lots of baby kittens.

I don't want to think about never seeing Napoleon again.

Harriet is out with the Colonel. I said that I was ill, and she believed me. I have stuffed my bolster under the covers in my bed in case they look in on me when they come home. With luck, if they do not look too closely, I shall not be missed till morning. There is a note pinned to my pillow for when they do find me gone—my final revenge on Wickham! I have told Harriet that we have run away to be married. I almost died when I thought of that. He is still away, and cannot contradict it, and Harriet will believe it, too—she is so convinced that I am in love with him! That will throw them off the scent! By the time he returns to town, I will be far away and it will be too late.

Farewell, Market Street. Farewell, dear Brighton, your beach and your bathing machines, your assembly rooms and library and shops, your crooked old cottages and fine new buildings! Farewell, Harriet and Denny and Carter and Colonel Forster and Theo and Esther!

Farewell, Wickham . . .

I am going to creep down the dark, narrow stairs and through the street that smells of fish, and walk close to the wall with my face hidden by the hood of my cloak, and I will not look up or back until I reach the Coach and Anchor and take my place in the London stage beside Alaric. Soon I will be Lydia, Comtesse de Fombelle . . .

The clock has chimed. It is half-past eight.

It is time.

⚬⚬ LATER STILL . . . ⚬⚬

How can everything change so fast? Earlier it was all so clear. Now everything has gone wrong.

It is eleven o'clock, and I am sick with anticipation. I am writing this in hiding, sheltered on the beach beside a fisherman's upturned boat, writing by the light of the moon.

It is only a few minutes' walk from Market Street to the Coach and Anchor. In my eagerness, I arrived early. The London coach was still being readied, and the yard was all bustle and shouting. A fine mizzle was falling, but I dared not go inside in case someone recognized me. I lurked in the shadows instead, with my bag at my feet and my cloak pulled close about my face. I could hardly breathe from excitement.

The horses were brought from the stables and hitched. The coachman came out of the inn, rubbing his hands, his face still red from his supper, and took his seat. The postbag was stowed, trunks and parcels secured.

Alaric did not come—he did not come, and he did not come.

The postilion mounted one of the front horses. An elderly gentleman in an old-fashioned cloak took his place in the coach.

Where was Alaric? Oh, where was he?

A hand fell on my shoulder, making me cry out.

"Shh!" a voice whispered.

I turned. It was *Wickham*!

"What are *you* doing here?" I hissed. "I thought you were gone away."

"That's a fine way to greet a fellow! I could ask you the same thing."

Wickham, returned . . . The letter lying on my pillow . . . Harriet would know that I had lied. He was going to ruin everything!

"You were meant to be away for days!" I accused him.

"Unfinished business drew me back early." Did he mean Miss Lovett? Did he know that she was leaving?

"London, London! Last call for London!" the coachman cried.

Oh, where was Alaric?

And now the coachman was grunting, "Ho!" and the horses were setting off with a great shaking and creaking.

He had still not come! I stifled a cry and stumbled out of the shadows. As Wickham caught me, his eyes fell on the bag at my feet.

"Lydia, what is this?"

"Oh, do not ask, do not ask!"

"Lydia!" He glanced around to make sure no one was watching, then took me by the arm and led me to a dark corner of the yard, where he sat me upon a bale of straw and made me tell him everything.

"They are leaving? With Miss Lovett?" So he hadn't known! His face was pale in the darkness, his features drawn. "Are you sure?"

"Quite sure! Why would I make it up? Oh, Wickham!"

"Then I have lost." He sighed. "And I felt so sure that this time I might win."

He dropped onto the bale beside me and hunched over his knees, deep in thought. I have never seen Wickham look so despondent. I remembered what Harriet had said—about his mountains of debts, and the Colonel running out of patience.

"We have both lost." I began to cry. I tried to stop myself, but the tears just came. Wickham reached out absently and squeezed my hand.

"Maybe he has sent word," I whispered. "Wickham, will you go into the inn and ask?"

"Of course I will."

I wrapped my cloak closer about me, retreated farther into the shadows, and waited. I fancied there was a renewed spring to his step when he came out, but he shook his head as he approached.

"Nothing," he said.

"What shall I do?"

"Lydia, let me take you home."

Home! I started. Glanced up at the clock. A quarter past nine. Harriet would still be out. I could creep back in and unpack my things, and she would never know that I had nearly escaped . . . And then what? A few more weeks of Brighton and parties, and then home to Longbourn, doubtless to die an old maid, never seeing the world and destined to live the rest of my days with my sisters?

I would not give up so easily.

"I'm not going home," I said. "I'm going to find Alaric."

"What? Lydia, how?"

"You have to help me get to Tara."

"Lydia, this is madness! Think what you risk—your reputation, ruin . . ."

"Oh, that word!" I actually stamped my foot. "I will not be ruined. If I can but talk to Alaric, I know that all will be well. Something has detained him at Tara—his awful sister, no doubt."

"Can it not wait until tomorrow?"

"He leaves tomorrow for Shropshire!"

"And if you fail, Lydia? If he refuses to see you, if his sister wins?"

"Take me to Tara, Wickham," I begged. "Help me get to him before it is too late!"

"How will we get there?"

"On horseback, of course!"

"But it's dark . . ."

"It's a full moon!"

"But—"

Wickham sighed. I could tell that he was wavering.

"*Please*, Wickham . . ."

"Oh, very well, wait here."

Back he went into the inn, taking my valise. Some minutes

later he came out again and, shielding me from view, led me around to the side of the inn, where a boy waited with two saddled horses.

"You will have to ride like a man," he said. "Will you manage that? I could not risk asking for a sidesaddle. The boy will not talk, for I have paid him handsomely, but the fewer people know a lady is riding about in the dead of night, the better."

"I will do anything it takes," I replied.

∽∾

I confess, as Wickham and I rode out together, I did temporarily forget about eloping and Southampton and India. Riding astride is completely different from riding sidesaddle, and at first I was convinced that without my front knee wrapped about the high pommel, I would slip off. But Wickham is a good teacher—I had forgotten that—and I soon adjusted. He led and I followed, my horse nudging his. We took the sea road out of town to avoid detection. There is a bridle path on the cliff that Wickham knows, which connects eventually with the road to Tara. It was slow, hard riding at first. The path was sunken and rocky, muddy, too, from the afternoon's rain. The horses picked their way carefully through the roots of the trees that arched high above us, their tall branches silhouetted against the night sky. But when we reached the high ground . . . when the empty road stretched out before us like a ribbon beneath the high moon . . . Wickham took off at a gallop. I screamed, and my horse followed.

Wind whipped past me. Tears streamed from my eyes, my

cloak billowed behind me. It was . . . oh, it was like swimming in the open sea, but even better! The thundering hooves, the speed— the danger and the excitement!

All too soon we slowed. "I seem to remember I owed you a ride!" Wickham laughed. "I had not imagined it in these circumstances."

"Why did we stop?" I asked breathlessly.

"Look where we are." He pointed to the side of the road. We were at the elephant gates.

Wickham said, "All right, Lydia, what's the plan?"

"We creep up to the house," I said, trying to sound confident.

"And then? Are you planning to climb up to his window?"

"Don't be ridiculous!" I blanched, thinking of Alaric's study right at the top of the house.

"Do you want me to come with you?" Wickham asked, and I nodded.

We tethered the horses in a copse, and crept together down the moonlit drive.

"Life is never dull with you, is it?" he whispered.

"Shh!"

"Admit it—you are enjoying the adventure!"

We had arrived at the stables, all closed up for the night. I motioned at Wickham to stop.

"I don't like to leave you," he said.

"I will call if I need help. It will be worse if they see you."

On I went, alone. Through the tunnel of trees, past the

turning circle and rosemary and the roses. The India palace gleamed silver in the moonlight. Everything was still after the storm. Not a rustle—not even the sound of Patch barking.

I was breathless again, hot and cold with a mounting dread.

I slipped round the side of the house—the furniture was gone from the terrace—ran down the twisted, narrow path to the summerhouse—peered in through the window . . . It was empty. The manikins, the bolts of cloth, the trays of pins and buttons . . . They were all gone.

I sank to the ground and sat for a long time on the cold damp stone, my back against the summerhouse wall, staring across the dark and empty garden. At some point, Wickham joined me. I did not look up.

"The stables are empty," he said. "I looked in through a window. The trap is there, but no horses."

"They have already left," I said dully.

I shivered. Wickham put his arm around me and drew me to him. I rested my head on his shoulder.

"It is his sister's doing," I said. "She will have found out somehow, and made them all leave. She thinks I am . . ." *Vain, ignorant, idle, and absolutely uncontrolled* . . . I gave a sob of anger. Why does everyone but Alaric think so little of me?

"Come on," Wickham said. "You can't stay here."

He helped me to my feet. As I followed him up the path to the terrace, I began to *shake* with anger against the whole world— Theo for taking away Alaric, Lizzy for her unkind words, Mary for always being so superior, Mr. Collins for *his* patronizing remarks, and my father, for always favoring my sisters over me . . .

I will show them, I thought. I will show the whole lot of them. I will find Alaric and I will make him marry me *at once* and then I will march him to Longbourn, and if I fall and ruin myself in the process at least I will have tried.

"Lydia?" Wickham tugged at my arm. "We have to go."

I stopped to look at the sea. The moon was low on the water, its reflection a silvery path.

"This is my only chance," I said.

"There will be other chances, Lydia . . . Other proposals."

"Not as good as this one."

A pause, and then Wickham asked, "So what do we do now?"

"Now," I said, "we go to London."

I lied to Wickham to convince him to come with me. It is wrong, I know, but I don't care. I cannot very well travel alone. I told him that I had spoken with Esther—that she begged me to tell him she would marry him, if only he would go after her. And he believed me.

I did not tell him about the note I had left for Harriet.

Once Alaric sees me, his sister will have no power over him. I know that he will remember India, and all the promises he made. Soon, the cold gray Channel will become the bright blue of the Indian Ocean, the thin moonlight that I am writing by will be the blazing sun of the tropics. There will be white scrubbed decks and full sails, and a dear little cabin with a round porthole and furniture screwed down to stop it being tossed about during a storm, like in the travel book the librarian gave me. There will be flying fish and dolphins and porpoises and whales, and it will all be wonderful.

Wickham left while I was writing, and has just returned from the inn. He has found a chaise to take us to London. No alarm has been raised. No one is yet looking for me.

SUNDAY, 19TH JULY

We are in London! It is not a bit as I imagined it—smart gentlemen and ladies riding about in fine carriages, and everyone vastly elegant. This inn is noisy and dirty, and it smells bad, and there are people everywhere, shouting in strange harsh London voices. I want to go out and explore, but Wickham says I must stay hidden. I am writing from the room of the inn where Wickham has left me. He has gone out to see some people who can help us—people who can lend him money, for we spent the last of ours on a hackney carriage from Clapham (so that anyone pursuing us might lose our trail, he explained).

The news from Grosvenor Square was not good. Wickham

went to make discreet enquiries as soon as we arrived, to work out a plan for how to meet Alaric, but "They are not here," he informed me when he returned. "I asked a tradesman—a fruit seller—if he could point out the home of Mrs. Lovett and I watched it for several hours, but no one came in or out. In the end, I tipped my fruit-selling friend to make enquiries, under the pretense of trying to sell his apples."

"And?"

"The family was expected, but never came. The housekeeper received word last night that they have all gone straight into Shropshire."

The serving girl brought ale. We both drank, lost in thought.

"Where exactly *is* Shropshire?" I asked.

"A long way northwest of here. Some two days' travel, perhaps."

"North?" I brightened. "Near Scotland?"

"Not really. Closer than London, I suppose."

"Then let us go to Shropshire!"

"Lydia . . ."

"Wickham! Think of Miss Lovett!"

We leave in the morning—if Wickham can get enough money . . .

FRIDAY, 24TH JULY

After days of traveling, we are finally approaching Shropshire. In another few hours' travel, Wickham says, we shall reach Mapperton Abbas, the village closest to Esther's grand estate. We have come a circuitous route—I wanted to go as fast as possible, but Wickham advised caution. There was nothing to be gained from charging after the Comte and Miss Lovett, and everything to be lost by being found, for by now people must be looking for us. Our route has taken us across country, through countless cities and villages. We have traveled by coach and hackney carriage, we have ridden in a farmer's cart, we have even done a stretch of road on foot, Wickham carrying my valise and urging me forward by teaching me sailors' songs he learned when he was at sea. It is a far cry from *Romeo and Juliet*, but it passes the time—no, I will be fair. It is a far cry from Shakespeare, but it makes me laugh.

We take one room wherever we stop, to save money. Wickham sleeps on the floor and I take the bed. At first I worried that he might try to—well, *ruin* me. He is not exactly as gentlemanly as Alaric—the very fact that he is here with me at all is proof of *that*. But he has behaved very well. How much more space he takes up than Kitty! How much louder his breathing, his snores, and every other sound! He kicks off his boots and they fly halfway across the room. Throws his coat on a chair and causes it to rock. Falls onto the bed (before taking to the floor) and makes the pillows fly. He paces continuously. He burps when he drinks beer.

Yet for all that, when he is sleeping, he looks strangely vulnerable. He takes a blanket, but always throws it off. He lies on his back with his arms behind his head, and his hair, which he keeps so carefully swept back during the day, falls across his face. The first night, I watched it rise and fall softly with his breath. Up and down, up and down . . . He opened his eyes and saw me watching.

"Lydia?"

"You should lie on your side," I said. "Maybe that way you would snore less."

At night, in these unfamiliar places, I stare out of the open window and try to picture those scrubbed decks, that bright blue sea. Sometimes what we are doing seems impossible, but we have come too far to turn back. If I do not succeed with Alaric, it will be Longbourn and virtual imprisonment for me, and Wickham says he cannot return to the regiment now that he has run away with me. His whole future now rests, he says, on marrying Miss Lovett. He still does not know that I have lied to him. I am trying not to think about how that makes me feel.

"Was I snoring again?" Wickham asked last night as we lay in darkness.

"Snoring? Not at all."

"And yet you are still awake."

I rolled to the edge of the bed and looked down at where he lay, tangled in his blanket.

"What if we are wrong?" I asked. "What if Alaric will not come away with me? What will happen to me then?"

"This count of yours, is he a man of honor?"

"Oh, most definitely!"

"And he made you a promise?"

"I think so," I said.

"Then he will keep it. And you have nothing to fear."

"He once told me that he and his sister had promised always to look after each other," I said. "What of that, if he comes away with me?"

"You have to fight, Lydia," he murmured.

"I'm frightened," I whispered.

"I know."

"Wickham?"

"Go to sleep, Lydia."

"The first time we met—in the street at Meryton—you told

me you had sailed the Mediterranean on a ship called the *Lydia*. Do you remember? Was that true?"

"Of course it was true! What do you take me for, a liar?"

I didn't dignify that with an answer. "What were you doing on a ship?"

"I had a monstrous gambling debt to pay off to her captain, and no means of doing so other than slaving away for six months on his blasted merchant vessel."

I smiled in the darkness at the thought.

"Wickham?"

"For God's sake, what?"

I fell asleep listening to him telling me about the Mediterranean.

SATURDAY, 25TH JULY

We have arrived at Mapperton Abbas. They are here—
so close! The innkeeper confirmed it—the whole
family, Esther and Mrs. Lovett, Theo and Alaric,
even the maid Marie.

Esther's estate is ENORMOUS. I don't know what Denny
was thinking when he said it was small—it is at least as big as
Netherfield. And I bet if Shakespeare himself were to see it,
he would spontaneously write whole volumes of sonnets in its
praise, because it is lovely. The house is built of pale gray stone
and sits in a wide sunny valley surrounded by hills. There are meadows full of flowers and sheep, and paddocks with fat horses, and
dairy cows to make Mr. Collins weep. Around the house there

are white roses, and lavender and thyme and rosemary and mar-
joram, and there are woods with cuckoos and blackbirds and
robins and doves. There are cotton-tailed bunnies in the fields,
and as Wickham and I walked over from the inn this morning,
I saw the long twitchy ears of a hare.

We went at daybreak, to survey the land before any of the
family rose. My boots and the hems of my dress and petticoat
were soaked with dew, but the sky was pink and blue and gold,
and the sun was already warm on our backs.

"It feels like the world is just beginning," I said to Wickham.

"The start of your new life." He smiled.

We walked through the woods on a white gravel path that
opened onto a lake, with a rowing boat painted a bright butter-
cup yellow. A wicked gleam entered Wickham's eye as he led me
to the water.

"We can't!" I said. "It is Esther's boat!"

"Esther will never know."

And oh, the joy of cutting through with your hand trailing
in the water, when the mist is still rising, and all about you there
are lilies, and frogs are jumping and birds are singing and a heron
is fishing among the reeds! If life could be always like that, I
would be absolutely happy.

My stomach rumbled as we rowed back to shore. Wickham
tied the boat to its mooring post and produced an apple and a
roll.

"Don't you want any?" I asked as I fell on them.

"I'm not hungry."

He lay back on the bank, careless of the morning dew, and tilted his face toward the sun.

"One day," he murmured, "all this could be yours."

"Not mine." I spat out an apple pip. It landed on his nose, and he brushed it away with an exasperated sigh. "It is Esther's, remember? I am for the tea plantation in India."

"I should like to see you on your plantation," Wickham said with a smile. "Riding about on your elephant."

I spat out another pip. "You can't ride about a plantation on an elephant," I scoffed. "It would trample everything. I shall have a dear little pony . . ."

"Someone's coming."

He was on his feet like a cat, dragging me away from the bank and into the shelter of the woods. I craned my neck to see.

"It is only a servant," Wickham whispered. "But the household is waking up. Come, let us go. We have an idea of how the land lies, and we can form a plan."

Wickham has gone, to find a housemaid he will bribe to take a message to Alaric. Oh God! I know now why Mamma complains so about her nerves—I think that I am going to be sick.

Alaric will come . . . I will speak to him . . . I will remind him . . . When he sees how far I have come, all that I have done . . . He will stand up to his sister. Yes, that is what will happen. We may not have to run away at all . . . He will see me, and he will tell Theo we are to be married, and we shall ride back to Longbourn together, and oh, how impressed they will all be.

When Alaric comes . . .

ꙮ THREE O'CLOCK ꙮ

I am sitting close to where we hid this morning, in the trees beside the lake, and I am waiting for him.

Wickham found a housemaid. She would not take a message for him, but she gave him some information, and Wickham told me exactly what to do.

"Every afternoon, at about half-past three, your young man goes to our yellow boat to read," he told me over luncheon—yet more bread and cheese. "The lake is easily reached from the village via a water meadow. There is a side gate, which is not locked during the day."

I still felt I was going to be sick.

"Thank you," I stammered. "You have been . . . You are actually very good to me. When all this ends well, I will tell Colonel Forster, and Father, and everybody . . . I will explain that this was all my idea . . ."

"I am not entirely unselfish in all this, you know. Miss Lovett is my principal reason for being here."

"Oh, you are . . ."

He put a finger to my lips. "Now, are you ready?" he asked. "Got your bonnet, your best frock, your walking shoes? Look at me—very pretty. No man could resist you, Miss Bennet, be he the King himself. Go, hurry—do not keep him waiting."

The path from the village wound round the meadows, bordered on either side by rushes and pink flowers, so tall in places they formed an arch over my head. Mapperton Abbas, with its cottages, church, inn, and pastures, disappeared from view, and for a few minutes I was completely alone in the wood. Then the vegetation thinned, the path disappeared, and I found myself standing before a gate. It was open, as Wickham had said it would be. I entered, walked a hundred yards to the lake, came to this bush, and waited. Am I ready? These last days have been so unreal. Part of me feels I never want them to end. But that is fear, nothing more.

It is just my nerves. The thing is not to let Theo see me. *She* is the enemy here. It is *she* who has taken Alaric away, I am quite sure of it. All will be well, as soon as I speak to him.

Someone is coming!

୭ SEVEN THIRTY ୭

It is all over. I am back at the inn—in bed, with a blanket about my shoulders and a glass of brandy on the table beside me brought by Wickham.

Alaric appeared at half-past three, just as the housemaid said he would, but he was not alone.

Esther Lovett walked beside him. No—Esther Lovett walked *with* him, on his arm.

I don't want to write of what came next. Of how Alaric rowed into the middle of the lake and then put down the oars. Of how the boat rocked as Esther came to sit beside him. Of how she rested her head on his shoulder—how he put his arm about her waist . . .

I gasped. My movement startled the heron, which took off in a great flapping of wings and came to settle with much commotion across the water from where I hid. I am mistaken, I thought. It is only a friendly gesture—between two people brokenhearted—a cousin consoling a cousin . . .

Alaric shaded his eyes to watch the heron. Esther pointed. The ring upon her finger glinted in the afternoon sun.

Esther—who never wears jewelry, who balked at the plainest pearl earrings before a dress ball—was wearing a *ring* . . .

And now it is all confirmed. Wickham found the housemaid again and made further inquiries, and learned that they are engaged, and plan to marry soon. Alaric is not to go to Oxford after all—or India, or anywhere else. He is to stay here with Esther and run the estate. They have great plans, the housemaid said, of improving the workers' cottages. She has seen his drawings, while she cleaned the study.

"It is all Theo's doing!" I sobbed in Wickham's arms. "I see it now—she never liked me, from the very first time we met at the Chalybeate Spa. He pressed me to come to Tara, but she did not want me to. And when we went swimming—I thought she was being so friendly, but she was trying to warn me off—she said she would do everything she could to protect him. I did not realize she meant from me! All the time, it has been Esther, Esther, Esther—all that time he was ill! He said himself it was only a little cold, but she forced him to stay behind so he shouldn't see me—so that he should see only her! And those dresses!" I burst into fresh sobs as I thought of Esther, tiny and ethereal, so much more elegant than me. "But why?" I wailed. "Why does she hate me so much?" Furious now, I paced about the room. Wickham put out a hand to still me, drew me to him.

"Lydia, calm down."

"He loves *me*!" I wailed. "And now he is engaged to Esther Lovett!"

There was a knock at the door. My heart beat wildly, thinking it might be him, but it was only a serving girl bringing supper. I burst into tears again and flung my arms about Wickham's neck.

"Darling Lydia," he murmured as the serving girl left. "We have to leave this place."

"I won't go home!" I cried.

"Well, there is nothing for either of us to gain by staying in Mapperton."

"You're right." I gazed over his shoulder out of the window. Evening already! Hours since I saw Alaric and Esther, but at this time of year the sun was a long way from setting. If the weather was like this at Longbourn, they would be taking tea out on the lawn—just as they always did, just as they always would. The very thought filled me with horror.

"What should I do?" I asked.

"I have to go to London," he said. "I must find some money, and it is the best place."

"I will go with you," I said.

"Lydia . . ."

"I shan't be a burden! I will think of something to do, soon enough. I don't know what yet, but I will think of something! And if I don't . . . well, if I don't, I suppose I will have to go back to Longbourn."

Wickham sighed. "Very well. I have spoken to the innkeeper. The next Shrewsbury coach passes on Monday afternoon. From there, it is but two days' traveling to London."

I felt drowsy after my tears. The food on the table was growing cold, but I did not move.

"Thank you," I said.

He tightened his arms about me. I fancy he even dropped a kiss on my head.

"I'm sorry about Esther," I said. With Wickham being so nice, I felt guiltier than ever for lying to him. "I promise that when I last saw her, she was still madly in love with you."

"Well, that's a comfort at least."

So off we go tomorrow, and I have to think of what to do . . . I have to think of something . . .

But what?

FRIDAY, 31ˢᵀ JULY

We have been in London two days now, sharing a room again at this inn in Holborn, and I am working on a plan.

It was Theo, of all people, who gave me the idea. The Comtesse de Fombelle, with her workroom and her silks, her grand ideas of becoming a famous designer of clothing, of one day having drawings published in *La Belle Assemblée*. Much as it pains me, I have re-read my account of our conversation on the beach. *I promised myself that we would never be poor again*, she said, *and that one day, I would show the world that a woman can be as good in business as any man.*

Why should the same not apply to me?

My new plan is to set up in business as a hatmaker. I know that I can make this work. It is true, I have meager capital—well, no capital at all, if I'm honest—but I have brought all my sewing things from Brighton, and all my ribbons, and Mamma is always saying how clever I am at making things—last winter, all those bonnets I re-trimmed! My green cape! Since we have been in London, I have walked every shopping street and arcade in the entire city, looking only at hat shops, and I am quite sure I can do it. All I need now is a shop, and stock and customers—which is daunting, but the key thing in all of this is to have the idea in the first place and to believe in yourself. That is what Wickham says. He thinks my plan is excellent, and has gone out now to find more money to help me make it happen. This afternoon, as soon as I have finished writing this, I am going to take apart my single bonnet, and reassemble it like one I saw in a shop this morning. I am going to cut up my pantaloons to cover it, with the ruffles all along the brim! Wickham was leaving as I was setting everything out, and he said, "You know, Lydia, I really admire you—what you are doing. You never give up, do you?"

"Never," I said. I did not even look up—too busy with my planning—but it made me feel warm inside.

How surprised everyone will be when they hear my plan! There will be an outcry at first, of course. Working in trade! Lydia, a businesswoman! Whoever heard of such a thing! She is bound to fail! But I shan't. I shall be a storming success, and all the best people will come to my shop—Theo herself, though I may refuse to serve her. There will be articles about me in *La Belle Assemblée*—even before there are even articles about Theo. Alaric will be sick to the teeth, knowing what sort of a person could once have been his wife, and I will make so much money suitors will be falling over themselves to propose to me, and everyone will think me monstrous remarkable . . .

Someone is outside—it must be Wickham, back already. Goodness, how much I have written! I must hide my diary before he sees me, lest he thinks I have not been working!

ཡ LATER ཡ

It was not Wickham. There were three strong raps at the door. Then, without waiting for an answer, it flew open—and Mr. Darcy strode in! He of all people!

His imperious gaze swept the room. I saw it suddenly as he did, the pantaloons spread across the table and my clothes strewn about the chairs, the narrow bed, Wickham's blankets on the floor, and I cringed.

"I have come to take you home!" he declared.

It's extremely hard not to feel small when you are confronted with someone like Mr. Darcy, but I did my best to appear outraged.

"I do not wish to go home," I said.

"Don't be silly," he snapped. "Your family is anxious. Your parents—your aunt and uncle—your sisters . . ."

Oh, I thought. My sisters! *That* is why he is here . . .

"Where is he?" said Mr. Darcy. "Wickham . . . where has he gone?"

"I have no idea," I said.

"Well, no matter. Pack your things, and come with me."

"I have already told you—I am not going back to Longbourn."

It seems quite unbelievable, but I swear that when I said that, Mr. Darcy doubled in size. He is a big man anyway, but his anger seemed to fill the room, and his dark eyes were like blazing coal.

"I am not taking you to Longbourn," he said. "We are going to your uncle Gardiner at Gracechurch Street. He will decide what is to be done with you."

"My uncle!"

"For God's sake, Lydia!" I noticed that he had dropped the "Miss." "How can you think to stay here with this man! If you only knew what he is capable of—what he has done! Come home with me now, and all will be well. Your family will protect you. *I* will protect you, for the sake of . . . for the sake of . . ."

He could not say it. He sat down heavily upon the sofa, and frowned at me. I glared back. For some time, we appeared to be in a deadlock. Then there were more footsteps outside, the door was flung open—and Wickham entered.

"Good Lord!" he cried. "You here, Darcy—what are you doing in my room?"

"I have come to take Miss Lydia," said that gentleman in tones of ice.

Wickham crossed the room to stand by me—put his arms about me—drew me to him. What was he doing?

"You will have to kill me first," he said.

Darcy actually rolled his eyes. "No one is going to kill anyone," he said. "Miss Lydia, come with me. If this is to be the shape of things, let us go to my own home for now."

"To *your* home?"

"You had better go with him, my love," Wickham said, sighing. "I will follow you shortly."

"Go with him? Wickham! What are you talking about?"

He pulled me to one side, put his hands on my shoulders, and looked straight into my eyes. "Lydia," he whispered, "do you trust me?"

"No."

A faint trace of a smile, then, "Well, you should."

"She will go with you," he said, turning to Darcy. "Though I must tell you neither of us appreciates your high-handed tactics."

Five minutes later, I was in a carriage, on my way to Mr. Darcy's house.

It is the grandest house I have ever stayed in, all silent and cold with closed-off rooms and marble everywhere. My very bedroom is the size of an entire floor at Longbourn, which is just as well because I refuse to leave it.

MONDAY, 3RD AUGUST

Today they brought me to my uncle's house, which is narrow and dark, with small rooms and a garden just big enough for a few shrubs. I will choke if I stay here any longer. I will *die*.

Nag, nag, nag . . . Aunt Gardiner never stops.

"What were you thinking?"

"How could you do this to your family?"

"Have you and Wickham—have you—oh, never mind if you have or not! You must marry him, and fast!"

"Why on earth would I marry Wickham?" I asked.

"Impossible girl! Everyone knows you are in love with

him . . . Kitty says your letters are full of him, and a mysterious project!"

"Kitty!" I sighed.

"Were you planning on living forever in sin? Were you never going to marry him?"

"Oh, I daresay we would have gotten round to it sooner or later, maybe," I snapped, to shock her into silence.

"I am going to fetch your uncle."

In came my uncle, with my aunt right behind him.

"You *must* marry him! Think of your sisters!"

"Who will marry them, when you are such a disgrace?"

"Be careful, Lydia, that they do not cast you off."

My family would not cast me off—would they? A memory— Aunt Philips's visit to Longbourn when the regiment first came to Meryton, the whispered conversation about Annie Atwood, who ran off with a soldier and was never spoken of again. Nothing has happened between Wickham and me, nothing— unless you count the running away—the shared rooms . . . But I have lost . . . I risked everything, and have lost! Perhaps if I explained, if I told them it was not as they all thought . . . Would it be better to know that I ran after Alaric?

My dreams of opening a shop—of becoming a businesswoman—how silly they seem now.

She never darkened their door again. Oh God! The picture of Napoleon has fallen out of my diary. Sweet Jane, drawing it for me! I read through the letters from my sisters—plain, cross, sour-faced Mary, who longs to see the Mediterranean and learn

German in Heidelberg! God, Mary, that is all I wanted, too! To see the world and live a little, to not always do what was expected! And now have I really ruined everything for you? And for Kitty, who longs only for a husband, and Jane still pining for Mr. Bingley, and Lizzy, who . . . oh Lord.

∾ LATER ∾

They brought Wickham to see me this afternoon, and left us alone together in their cold and gloomy parlor. He already looks different from the Wickham of the past two weeks—shaved and pomaded, his clothes pressed, his shirt laundered, as fresh and handsome as the very first time we came upon him in Meryton. I saw at once that someone must have given him money. Was it Mr. Darcy?

"Well now, Lydia," Wickham said. "Here is an interesting situation."

"What are you playing at?" I hissed.

"There's no need to . . ."

"Tell me!"

He sighed, reached into his coat pocket, and pulled out a letter—crumpled, the seal broken, and folded in four.

"What is this?"

"Just read, Lydia."

The note was addressed to me, and written in a hurried hand:

Lydia—all has been discovered. I was soaked to the skin when I returned home yesterday, and Theo guessed at once where I had been—there is only one person in all the world, you know, for whom I would get caught in the rain. We are to leave immediately. Do not judge her too harshly, Lydia. My stepfather— I tried to tell you on the beach. I am entirely to blame. God, I so wanted to be free! I so wanted _you_! My stepfather has lost all his money. He is a speculative man, given to grand gestures and unwise investments, and it has cost him his fortune. This is the reason for Theo's feverish desire to start a business—and for other plans, too, which I cannot go into now. I am leaving this at the Coach and Anchor as we pass through, and pray that it will reach you in time.

Forever yours,

A. de Tombelle

I could not believe what I was reading.

"But they are—I thought that they were rich . . ."

Wickham did not reply.

I so wanted to be free . . . I so wanted you . . .

The old black trap—only one servant—the dilapidated house! The frayed hem of Theo's green dress, the rip in Alaric's jacket! The clues had all been there—and I had thought them all eccentricities! Even Theo and her dressmaking business—I could see her now, philosophizing after our swim—I never thought she actually needed the money. And there was Mrs. Lovett and her social aspirations, with all the money she needed but still a tailor's daughter. A title—any title—would elevate her once and for all, and finally cut the ties to her past.

I never stood a chance.

"They are no different from the rest," I whispered.

"Few people are, when it comes to rank and money."

"And you!" I cried. "You found this letter at the Coach and Anchor! And yet you said nothing—you let me run after him to Shropshire! Did you really think you could stop this—that you could get Esther back?"

He drew up a chair and came to sit before me.

"I will be honest with you, Lydia. I have known of John Shelton's economic difficulties for some weeks."

"What? How?"

"Let us say that I have taken an interest in the fortunes of the family since I first learned of *your* involvement with them."

"My involvement? But why?"

"Is it too difficult for you to believe, Lydia, that I care about you?"

"You don't care for people, Wickham, you care only for money!"

"I do care for money," Wickham said. "As does any sensible person. But it is not fair to say that is all I care about. Lydia, listen to me carefully. Darcy has paid off my debts and bought me a commission with a new regiment, in the North. For reasons you must have guessed, he is anxious that no news of this escapade should get about. You have my promise that not a word of our adventure shall pass my lips, though I cannot speak for others. That unfortunate note you left Harriet Forster . . ."

Darcy! My mind raced, furiously. Back to the night at the New Theatre in Brighton—*Mr. Darcy seemed very affected when he saw you, Lydia . . . Darcy always gets what he wants . . .*

Do you trust me? Wickham said when Mr. Darcy found us.

I buried my head in my hands, trying to go over everything that has happened.

"You knew from the moment you saw me with Mr. Darcy that I could be useful to you . . ." I said. "But you did not know how. Then, when you found Alaric's letter . . ." I gazed at him, horrified. "Did you know then that he would marry Esther?"

"I had heard enough of the Comte and Comtesse's financial affairs to suspect his sister at least of desiring the outcome," he admitted.

Oh, what a fool I had been! Everything made sense now. Wickham did not come with me to Shropshire to pursue Esther—he came to discredit *me* . . . to ruin *me* . . . And I had fallen for his talk *again*, as so many had before me . . .

Darcy has paid off my debts . . .

"You knew that Mr. Darcy would follow us, to avoid a scandal, because of the harm it would do to Lizzy. You knew that he

311

would want to save her family from disgrace . . . You pretended all was not lost so that I would run away with you . . . And my business—my hat shop—you wanted to keep me in London until we were discovered; you never truly believed I could . . ."

I squeezed my eyes shut to stop my tears.

"How did you know I would insist on going to Shropshire?"

"I didn't. My first thought on finding the letter, you will remember, was to take you home to Market Street. But I am a gambler, Lydia. I play my cards as they are dealt."

"You cheat," I hissed. "And you played me."

"Did not you play me, too, when you lied about Esther Lovett? You did lie, didn't you?"

I stared out of the window.

"You are disgusted with me, because I seek to better my circumstances through marriage," Wickham said. "But look around you, Lydia. Is not everyone doing the same? Is it not what your mamma wants for her daughters—what the Comtesse de Fombelle wants for her brother and herself? Is it not what you have been doing yourself with the Comte de Fombelle?"

"That was different!"

"How?"

"I love him!"

"Do you?"

Wickham moved closer. His hazel eyes were dancing.

"I have known for some time, Lydia, that you and I would be good for each other. No, do not be angry! I am not about to insult you by professing undying love. But be honest, now that the game is up and there is nothing left to hide. Do we not laugh together, and always have a good time?"

"Not always," I said sourly.

"I have to tell you that Darcy has offered a further sum if we are to marry. Your uncle and he have settled it."

"As if I were a horse or a cow!"

"It is the way of the world. You know that. None of us can escape it—but we can turn it to our advantage."

He seized my hands.

"Just imagine, Lydia!" he went on. "In Northumberland, there are great castles right on the sea. There are miles and miles of empty beaches, where you can swim for hours without seeing a soul, and afterward, you can gallop home across vast open country, with nothing but hills and sky between you and the Scottish borders, and in Newcastle, where I am to be stationed, the balls and assemblies are as fine as any you would find at Brighton. And it can all be yours, Lydia. No Harriet Forster, no older sisters, no mamma . . . Just you and me, against the world. What do you say? Does it not sound appealing? Do I not know you well?"

It was meant to be Scotland, Southampton, six months at sea. The blazing tropics, mangoes and guavas. And yet . . .

And the truth is, he does know me. Even if I hate to admit it . . . he does.

"If there were no money," I whispered, "you would not look at me twice."

"But there is money." How close he was standing! "What say you, Lydia? Will you take a chance?"

So close . . .

"Think of your sisters . . ."

His kiss was so soft. His lips brushed mine with the lightness of a butterfly landing, of silk running through fingers. And yet it produced such an explosion inside me . . . When he drew away, I clung to his neck.

Alaric's kiss was never like this.

"Very well," I whispered. "For my sisters . . ."

"And for you?"

I sighed and drew him back toward me again. "A little for me, too."

MONDAY, 17ᵀᴴ AUGUST

The news of my marriage was announced in the paper on the same day as Alaric and Esther's engagement, on the very same page. I tried to imagine their faces reading it. Was he a little ashamed of himself? A little sorry or jealous? And Esther, who was so in love with Wickham, and yet so quick to do what was asked of her—what would *she* make of it? Did she envy me, or pity me, knowing what Wickham is—a gambler and a chancer?

I find that I don't really care. He is *my* gambler and chancer now—my handsome, impossible gambler, and I am pinning my chances on him. I had no difficulty in guessing Theo's reaction— she, too, would not care. It has surprised me how much angrier

I have been with her than with her brother. Wickham is right—
we are all caught in this game, Alaric as much as anyone. But
Theo—for a short time, Theo with her workroom and dresses
and grand designs for the future made me think that anything
was possible. I suppose I cannot blame her for wanting the best
match for her brother, or the security it has brought her. She will
live with Alaric and Esther, knowing she will always have her
place at Mapperton. We are not so very different, she and I. We
are both fighters, and neither of us is the sort who drowns.

It was not the wedding most girls dream of. I did not wear
my white-and-gold gown from the Brighton ball, but my spotted
white muslin and one of the bonnets Harriet sent on with the
rest of my clothes from Brighton, and no one attended but my
aunt and uncle and Mr. Darcy, who breathed an audible sigh
when our vows were said, and no doubt is thinking of tearing
back to propose to Lizzy as I write. There have been no messages
from Longbourn, no congratulations except from Mamma, in a
letter dripping with relief at having at least *one* daughter married,
all about clothes. My uncle's carriage is being readied now to
take us to Epsom, where we shall take the coach. Soon enough
we shall be at Longbourn, and I shall see my family. I know very
well what they are all thinking of me. Father thinks me as silly as
ever. Jane is anxious, Mary dismissive, Kitty a little in awe of my
behavior. Lizzy is thoroughly disapproving. Mr. Darcy has made
me promise not to tell her what he has done for us. I can't think
why. If I were him, I would want the whole world to know, and
I still hope he will propose to her again. For all Darcy's help, I

don't think Wickham and I will ever be rich enough to support all my sisters when Mr. Collins inherits Longbourn. I may have to disobey him, and hint to Lizzy at what he has done. Otherwise she'll never change her mind. Yes, that is what I shall do—I shall drop it idly into the conversation at Longbourn, and she will fall madly in love with him and marry him out of gratitude. And when I go, I shall greet all my sisters with my head held high—for whatever they think of me, I *am* the first one married. And I know things—so many things!—that they do not. It seems quite extraordinary to me that I am still the youngest.

"Well, wife!" Wickham just came in, threaded his arm around my waist, and peered over my shoulder. "I hope you are writing about me."

I slammed my diary shut, and told him that there are some things even husbands are not allowed to see.

He left, laughing loudly, and bowed to a red-faced Aunt Gardiner, who was entering the room.

"Lydia! What are you doing, child? The carriage will be here soon!"

"By and by," I said, and now I am smiling as I write, because I am thinking of Juliet on her balcony calling "by and by" to her nurse, and of Alaric reading Shakespeare out loud at the Rookery in Brighton, and of what Mary would make of *that* if ever she knew of it. Better, perhaps, not to tell her. Better to let her keep Shakespeare for herself. Mine was only a passing knowledge, already almost forgotten.

Goodness, I have filled this entire diary! It seems as if no time has passed since Mary first gave it to me, and yet it has been more than a year. One day, perhaps, when the sea is too rough for bathing and the rain falls too hard on the vast Northumberland landscape, when Wickham is out on exercises and I am too tired for an assembly, I will read it again from the beginning, and how it will make me laugh! I may even read Shakespeare again, too. Or perhaps, which is more likely, I will pick up the latest edition of *La Belle Assemblée*. And there will be Theo's drawings in it, the long-awaited pelisse maybe, English oak leaves lined with Indian leopard.

One day, Wickham and I may yet make that voyage to India. We will sail for months on waters so clear I can see shipwrecks and treasure at the bottom of the sea, and when I arrive there will be elephants and mangoes and mynah birds, and we will gallop up into the hills together to the tea plantations and watch the hills turn blue in the afternoon light, and I will think about what almost was. And I will have my daughter with me—a brilliant daughter, in a dress worthy of the Comtesse de Fombelle, as clever as she is beautiful, who will read books and ride horses and will not be afraid of anything—and I will tell her that the lot of women need not be so different from that of men, and hope that by then it will be true.

But I am not going to think about that now.

∽ THE END ∽

AFTERWORD

When the idea for this book was first mooted by the team at Chicken House, I sought advice from an academic friend who specializes in the works of Jane Austen. Lydia, who in my mind was already a living, breathing person, was skipping about, twirling her bonnet and crying "At last! My side of the story!" but I was less certain.

"Don't even try and copy Jane Austen," my friend said. "Just be yourself, be respectful, and know that whatever you do, she is sitting up there in author–heaven laughing at you."

I have done my very best to be respectful, not least in mapping the timeline of my story on *Pride and Prejudice*, but have had to make a few conscious decisions concerning dates. Jane Austen wrote her novel over ten years. While we are never told in which year *Pride and Prejudice* is set, the presence of military encampments in Brighton suggests it was in the mid-1790s (after which the military were housed in barracks). However, I wanted Alaric and Theo to have escaped the French Revolution, and for his memories of this event to be much vaguer than his sister's. For this reason, I chose to set my book toward the latter part of *Pride and Prejudice*'s gestation period. The year 1811 was the first of the Regency period, which saw George, Prince of Wales, rule as proxy for his father, George III. The Prince of Wales was a great fan of Brighton and one of the chief reasons the resort became so vastly fashionable. It seemed a fitting year in which to begin Lydia's story.

The timing of Lydia's flight with Wickham is ambiguous in Austen's novel. According to the dates of various letters, one timeline has them missing for a couple of weeks, but another, worked out through references in the text, suggests a longer period. I have chosen to go with the first, as it fits my story better.

I have also tried to be faithful to accounts of contemporary Brighton topography, but fear I have taken some liberties in my re-imagining of it. This, I am afraid, is what authors do. If you would like entirely reliable facts about Brighton at that time, I refer you to Sue Berry's fascinating *Georgian Brighton* (Phillimore & Co.); to The Keep (www.thekeep.info), which houses a fine collection of archive material; and to the local Brighton Museum (www.brightonmuseums.org.uk).

I have loved every minute of working on Lydia's story. As she herself would say, the whole process has been monstrous fun. And wherever Jane Austen may be, I hope she is in fits of laughter over it.

ACKNOWLEDGMENTS

My sincere thanks to Nicola Morrison for her precious advice on fashion and dancing. To Sean Gaston for pointing me in the direction of a mountain of invaluable reading on Jane Austen and her era. To the archivists at The Keep for the wonderful work they do in preserving archives of historical Brighton. To all the team at Chicken House for their creativity and efficiency, and for giving me the opportunity to spend a happy year immersed in all things Austen. To my editor, Rachel Leyshon, for burning the midnight oil with me. To my agent, Catherine Clarke, for her usual incisiveness. To Elinor Bagenal, whose inspiring conversation lit the spark which ignited this whole project, and whose encouragement and enthusiasm have kept me going throughout. And to my family for cheerfully putting up with my disappearance into the early nineteenth century, and for welcoming me home.

ABOUT THE AUTHOR

Natasha Farrant is the author of *What We Did for Love* and the Diaries of Bluebell Gadsby series. Her writing was called "raucously funny" by the *New York Times*, and her books have been nominated for the Branford Boase Award, the Carnegie Medal, the Guardian Children's Fiction Prize, and the Queen of Teen award. She lives in London, England. Follow her on Twitter at @NatashaFarrant1.